PORTIA A. COSBY

# F.I.R.E.

## REIGNITED

### A NOVELLA

DISTINCT PUBLISHING

ATLANTA

ISBN-13: 978-0-9823013-5-7

PUBLISHER'S NOTE

This book is a work of fiction. Names, characters, places, and incidents are either the product of the author's vivid imagination or are used fictitiously, and any resemblance to actual persons, living or deceased, business establishments, events, or locales is entirely coincidental.

Cover design by The Final Wrap

Interior design by A Reader's Perspective

For information regarding special discounts for bulk purchases, please contact DISTINCT Publishing at ordernow@portiacosby.com.

Printed in the United States of America

# ACKNOWLEDGMENTS

For anyone who knows me personally, it's no surprise that I wrote this book. I grew up listening to and loving 90s R&B. I especially loved the girl groups. It was known among my friends that when certain songs came on the radio or if we were doing karaoke, I sang all of a particular group member's verses and adlibs. There was no compromising. LOL!

These characters had been developing in my head for about three years, and I'd written a few paragraphs here and there during that time. As I witnessed the resurgence of 90s culture, I knew it was time to introduce them to the masses. So, thank YOU for taking time to read their stories.

Amari: Thank you once again for sharing your time with Mommy's characters.

Rosie, Tamika, April, Star, Amica, and Lisa: Thank you, thank you, thank you for your feedback and encouragement as I hashed out this project.

Carla Dean: We're back at it! I appreciate how you "get" my writing. I'm blessed to have you as an editor, and thank you for working with me. I look forward to us working together on the next phase of F.I.R.E.

Nakia Laushaul (A Reader's Perspective): You gave this book the "feel" I needed it to have. I love working with like-minded creatives and professionals. Thank you for making the words pop with this design!

Nakia Laushaul (my friend and colleague): For believing in this project, for believing in me, for every-thing...thank you.

Rebecca Pau (The Final Wrap): What a pleasure to be connected with you! We were instantly on the same page (no pun intended) with my visions, and I thank you for bringing them to life.

Tracey Michae'l Lewis-Giggetts: I love you, Sis! Ten years later, you still have my back.

My Readers: Thank you for supporting my work throughout the years. Without you, this fifth book wouldn't exist. Your enthusiasm, encouragement, attendance at events, and not-so-subtle hints that you're waiting on another book from me ☺ have been invaluable and appreciated more than I can express. When I published my first novel, I never imagined so many people would care about "the people in my head." I never imagined I'd still be introducing you to said people ten years later. I'm forever grateful. What do you say we do this ten more years?

This book is dedicated to all R&B girl groups, past and present.

Thank you for blessing the world with your musical harmonies, even when there was dissonance within your personal relationships.

# FEISTY

# ICONIC

# REAL

# EXOTIC

**F.I.R.E.** is an American R&B girl group from Atlanta who crossed over to become an international R&B/pop sensation. Formed in 1997 and composed of four high school classmates **Paris**, **Shai**, **Reign**, and **KiKi**, the group experienced instant success with their debut single "No Games." Their first album, *Playing with Fire*, went platinum; and their other four albums attained multi-platinum status.

After a controversial challenge posed by Paris, all four group members also released solo projects in 2006. Though *All of Me* (Reign) and *Off Ki* (KiKi) went gold, Paris' album, *Passport,* went platinum; and Shai's *Just Me* went double-platinum, blowing their groupmates out of the water.

Personality conflicts, creative differences, and problems with addiction are rumored to have led to the group's split in 2008. During their time apart, Shai has become a  star in her own right, having released seven multi-platinum solo albums and counting. KiKi is a ten time Grammy-winning songwriter. Reign is a philanthropist and an advocate for children born with drug addiction. She occasionally performs acoustic sets in small venues, stating, "Music is in my blood. I'll never stop singing altogether." Paris disappeared from the public eye for about three years and reemerged married to rap superstar, Ricky V. She has been featured on numerous artists' projects but has not released new music of her own.

The group attempted a comeback in 2013 without Paris. They introduced a new member, **Simone**, but this wasn't well-received by fans. Simone was dismissed after performing in six shows and never recorded new music with F.I.R.E. When asked if all four original members will ever reunite, each artist gives no definitive answers; but it looks like F.I.R.E. will remain the old flame whose music still appeals to new listeners as the years go by.

Paris

xo

# WELCOME TO PARIS

**"So,** I have to ask," Melinda started. "How do your former group members feel about your new endeavor? Are they supportive?"

"Wait." I grabbed her wrist and gently pushed it back, along with the voice recorder she held in her hand. It seemed the juicier our conversation got, the closer her device got to my face, coming to within a couple inches of my mouth. "The last thing that hovered that close to my mouth belonged to my husband."

She laughed and apologized. Melinda Burton first interviewed me for her college newspaper almost twenty years ago; she was now writing for *Essence*

*Magazine.* We go way back and have always had a playful rapport.

"Well, one was with me when I gave the final approval," I continued. "One hasn't smelled it yet, but still bought a case to give to family members. I've heard nothing from the other person."

"Something tells me you won't give us the pleasure of matching the descriptions to the group members."

"It's not hard to tell. The same ones who shout me out on social media support me in real life."

She pursed her lips and her eyebrows rose to the middle of her forehead. "Did a drop of tea just spill on the floor?"

Keeping my mouth shut, I closed my eyes so Candy could apply my eyeshadow.

"What's next for Ms. Paris?" Melinda continued. "Your fans have missed you. I know you're not gonna stop here. Can we expect a clothing line? Joint album with the hubby?"

"I'm actually working on a book—my memoir. But, until that releases, all I can say is 'expect the unexpected.' What's most important after today's event is that I'm celebrating thirty-five years of life."

"And you certainly have a lot to celebrate. I can't wait to see what this next chapter of your life will bring."

Once we finished the interview, we chatted briefly about an upcoming women's expo she thought my team should look into and how she desperately wished F.I.R.E. would reunite for at least one show at Essence Festival. She knew the deal, though. I could only control Paris, and unless fans were okay with me just performing my verses of F.I.R.E.'s hits, they could stop waiting to exhale.

After Candy finished beating my face, Melinda's photographer snapped shots to accompany the article. My mama was going to be ecstatic. She was proud of my superstardom back in the day, but that wore off as time went on. *Essence Magazine*, however, was her jam, and she was looking forward to me being featured... alone.

When Melinda left, I stood at the vanity admiring the fiery auburn highlights that brought out the hazel in my eyes.

"Somebody's still been eating Waffle House after the club, I see." Jordan strutted in and placed his bag on the counter. He tugged on my dress, making sure the fabric contoured perfectly over my hips.

"Somebody's about to go stand in the unemployment line," I replied as I sent a quick text to my husband.

He snickered and finger-combed my hair while I danced to "The Weekend," one of F.I.R.E.'s biggest hits. Just like I wasn't paying him no mind, he wasn't paying me any either. He was confident he would still have a job by the end of the day, and I was certain all one hundred and thirty-two pounds of me were still intact.

Jordan is my boo. He's only been my assistant for two years, but I feel like we've known each other since middle school. Actually, he's kinda known *me* since he was in middle school, when he was a fan of my group. We like the same things when it comes to bags, shoes, TV shows, and men. Well, we only have the same taste in *some* men. Jordan wouldn't touch a man like my husband with a twenty-foot pole, while wearing gloves, and blindfolded.

"Is Ricky coming?" Candy asked as she powdered my sweaty nose again.

"No. He's at the studio," I replied.

"Aw, that stinks. Well, I know he's proud of you."

I smiled. He was. I didn't mind that I was rolling solo, though. Doing my event without Ricky present ensured that people were really there to see *me*. He's one of the hottest rappers in the game, so he can never join me at an appearance as my husband, Richard Valentine. The masses know him as Ricky V, and they'll chant that shit until he acknowledges them.

No shade, but I was a star before he even thought about making his first mixtape. As one-fourth of R&B girl group F.I.R.E., I have six platinum albums, three Grammys, six AMAs, five Billboard Awards, nine BET Awards, and twenty years of industry experience under my belt. I was collecting checks before most of my friends had work permits.

Sadly, our group broke up nine years ago because of Shai's selfish ass. Sharing the spotlight with the rest of us wasn't good enough for her. So, she decided to go solo and left me, Reign, and KiKi in the cold. We didn't know she was leaving the group or had been recording without us until she played her album for us a week before announcing its release date to the world. At that time, Zeke—her uncle and our manager—handed us a severance check and a pen to sign our STFU papers.

It's hell to go from making history with friends on a Thursday to being history on Friday. No heads up. No chance to prepare. No fucks given about what happened to her so-called friends while she was off to sashay across the stage alone, in a glittery leotard, wearing forty-five bundles of hair. We were left with a "thank you" for our services, while the person responsible for turning our worlds upside down was sitting on top of it *and* the Billboard 100 chart. If I sound bitter, it's because I am.

I had a four-year pity party and only invited about five guests. I changed my number, smoked weed or drank almost every day, and stayed in the house unless I was going to the doctor or had run out of liquor. During that time, I still received mad love from fans who shouted me out on social media or noticed me while I was out despite my disguises. Most begged for my autograph or a hug or a picture. Some just wanted to know what happened to F.I.RE. Since I couldn't tell them the truth because of the STFU papers, I would politely rush away and crawl back into my hole. That hurt me more than anything because I love our fans and have always felt they deserve to know the truth.

It was a pitiful existence for a while; and since it wasn't getting better, I wanted to end it. I now believe in angels, because Ricky swooped in at that moment and became more than just my cool-ass rapper friend. He saved me from myself when the only S.O.S. I was concerned with was the brand of scouring pads that would help get bloodstains out of the grout between my bathroom floor tiles. After all, I'd willed the house to my little sister, and somebody was gonna need to clean up my mess whether she decided to live in it or sell it. That's another story, though. Ricky reminded me who I am, and because of that, I'm finally doing something I dreamed of since my 11th grade AP chemistry class: debuting my own fragrance.

"The line is out the door and down the walkway past Victoria's Secret!" one of the Macy's associates said after flinging back the privacy curtain to the makeshift dressing space.

I ceased primping in the mirror and turned to her. "That's amazing!" I responded with a bashful giggle. "I hope we have enough perfume."

"Well, it's never a bad thing to sell out. Mrs. Valentine, I'm so glad you agreed to do your in-store here with us. I've been a fan since F.I.R.E. first came out." The associate was beaming.

"Call me Paris. And I appreciate you. Matter of fact…" I motioned for her to come over. "Jordan, can you take a picture of us? What's your name, boo?"

She stood next to me, trembling, but managed to utter, "Angela."

"Are you nervous? Don't be nervous!" I pulled her close, and we posed for my cellphone camera. "You smell good." I winked, and she laughed.

"This fragrance is everything," she replied, before asking if we could take a selfie using her phone.

I obliged. My fans got me to where I was before, and they were going to get me there again. Taking five seconds to make their day was a miniscule deed compared to them helping me make my dreams a reality. Before Angela returned to the fragrance counter, she made sure to post our picture on all her social media accounts. Hashtag: LIT.

LIT was the name of the perfume I'd created with a fine-ass German chemist named Friedrich. I met Friedrich at a bar in London. Ricky has done numerous shows in the city over the years, and the small space has become my spot whenever I accompany him.

One evening, Friedrich sat on the stool next to me and offered to buy me a drink. Not long after we exchanged brief, subtle life stories, he complimented me on how wonderful I smelled and asked what I was wearing. At first, I thought he was flirting, but after he revealed his occupation, I shared with him that I had mixed some oils to create an original scent. Impressed, he passed his business card to me and asked me to call him the next day. Our legal teams worked out the logistics of our partnership, and off to the lab he went. It took us about a year to perfect the fragrance. I wanted it to smell like my personality: feisty, sexy, fun, carefree, and girly-with-a-hint-of-dude. Friedrich made it happen.

"Okay. It's showtime, Superstar!" Jordan said after receiving a text.

"I'm back, bitches," I muttered under my breath before exiting the dressing area with my favorite F.I.R.E. song, "Party Like…," playing as my theme music.

Two security guards flanked my sides, escorting me toward a table set up in the middle of the fragrance section. I waved and blew kisses to the sea of supporters who screamed my name while holding up photos and CDs. Some even managed to graze my skin as I maneuvered through a narrower space.

Angela handed me a mic when I reached the table. Before saying a word, I stood still and inhaled the energy of the place for a few seconds. Then, "What's good, L.A.? We lit!" I danced to the beat, further hyping the crowd, further hyping myself. I missed this. When my verse blasted through the speakers, I instinctively sang along to half of it. I wanted to continue grooving, but the in-store was scheduled to last only two hours. So, we needed to get started.

"Alright, alright. Y'all gon' get us kicked outta here. Got me up here cuttin' up." I smirked. "I have to thank each and every one of you for coming out today. You'll never understand what this means to me. Many people don't know this about me, but if I wasn't in the music industry, I'd probably be in a lab somewhere making secret potions and blowing up stuff. I was heavily involved in the creation of this fragrance, and I hope you love it as much as I do."

I rested my hand on my chest as random people professed their love for me.

"Oh! A couple things: Yes, I'll take pictures, and no, I can't sign CDs and t-shirts. I can only sign the perfume boxes. Not my rules, so don't be on social media talkin' shit about me bein' stuck up. K? Let's get it."

I started to sit, but then stood up straight again and did a three-sixty scan around the area.

"Oh, and to whoever grabbed my booty on my way in, you need to purchase five bottles. You ain't slick."

Laughter erupted, and I took my seat.

The event was going well. Fans asked the usual questions about F.I.R.E. making a comeback. Some asked where Ricky was or if I was going to release another solo album. I met children who were named after me, half-listened to fans who had the event confused with an *American Idol* audition, politely declined male fans' attempts to pass their numbers, and gave hugs to super fans I recognized from years ago. An hour in, my cheeks were sore from smiling and laughing.

That smile quickly turned into a scowl when "Fake Love to Me" began playing in the background. I stopped mid-conversation with Nia from Tucson and whipped my head in the direction of Jordan and two Macy's reps. I pointed my finger in the air and bucked my eyes. Jordan squinted, looking for clarity. The expression on his face changed once he recognized the melody. He looked left and right, then grabbed a male rep by his arm and spoke intently. As they conversed, Jordan's arms flailed, fingers pointed, and his neck held a strong forty-five degree angle. After a little back and forth, he pulled out what I assumed to be my contract from his bag.

"This was my song! Do you ever hear from him?" Nia asked while waiting for me to sign her merchandise.

She was referring to the man singing—my ex, YB. "Fake Love to Me" was one of five duos we had collaborated on.

I looked down at my dress to see if my heartbeat was visible. *Hell no, I don't hear from him anymore nor do I want to.* Our relationship was destructive to my mind, body, and soul. I almost let it destroy my career. We loved each other publicly and passionately. We were one of music's hottest couples. However, a lot of pressure came from that heat, and our relationship became explosive. I will always have love for Brandon, but from afar—farther than my restraining order once dictated.

He's a gifted artist. I've been able to tolerate most of his music but consciously stayed away from our joint projects because many of them were based on our courtship. I never imagined I would have such an intense physiological reaction if I happened to hear one, though.

I wiped the sweat from my hand onto the chair's fabric and picked up my Sharpie.

"Now why would I hear from him?" I replied with a fake smile.

After I signed the fragrance box and took a picture, I signaled for the next person in line to wait before approaching the table.

Jordan was no longer in sight. The song was still playing. My hand was trembling like I had an acute case of Parkinson's, and my heart felt like it was punching my rib cage. I picked up the mic and spoke politely but matter-of-factly.

"Excuse me. Can someone please turn that shit off? Now."

That night, multiple videos of my snippy request surfaced on popular entertainment blogs, Instagram, and Twitter. The sound bite was playing nationwide on urban radio stations by the next morning. #LIT was trending along with #turnthatshitoff, #dayumYB, and #ParisValentine. I was getting the attention I'd hoped for, just not for the reasons listed in my business plan.

If Nia from Tucson is still wondering, I did hear from Brandon. Well, Debra, my manager, heard from him. He was "checking on" me because he didn't feel my reaction to hearing our song should have been that serious. She didn't share the other part with me, but Jordan's eavesdropping ass did. Apparently, Brandon speculated that I used him for publicity because his career is still popping and I knew people who were recording would post footage of the moment. *Cocky ass.*

He even posted a tweet to back up his delusion.

> **Young Boi Brandon** @therealYB100
> U welcome, boo.

Because I can't let anybody think they chumped me, I disregarded my team's advice to ignore him. Since he wanted my attention and I had a little to spare, I tweeted, too.

> **Paris Valentine** @FIREinParis
> Young Bois do young shit, even when they're old AF. Grow up. #turnthatshitoff

Debra chastised me via phone, but only after she stopped laughing. Ricky told me not to respond again because if Brandon got out of pocket and he had to get involved, things wouldn't be pretty. My baby doesn't have Twitter fingers. He lays hands in real life. Not wanting it to come to that, I promised I was done. Besides, I had better things to do, like celebrate my upcoming birthday. Brandon was the master of ruining my mood back in the day, but those days were over.

Ricky insisted I wear the see-through Gucci dress he surprised me with that morning. I told him it wasn't appropriate for the restaurant he was taking me to and that I planned to wear it for my party once we returned to Atlanta the next day. I've never been the type to shy away from inappropriate attire or activity, but I didn't want to waste the wear at a seafood restaurant when it could be seen by more people at an actual event. Out of nowhere, our debate turned into a full-fledged argument, with him telling me that he wanted me to wear the dress because we were going to a club afterward. He was frustrated because he wanted me to just go with the flow, and I was clogging shit up. Touché.

When I walked down the steps, Ricky forgot why he was mad. He tucked his bottom lip between his teeth and kept his eyes glued on my body. Everything was visible except my cookie jar and nipples. I won't lie and say I didn't want to holler at my damn self when I looked in the mirror. The black lace laid like it was painted on me, accentuating every curve. Almost thirty-five, I still looked like a snack, and Ricky looked ready to devour me.

Instead, we feasted on branzino and king crab on Catch LA's rooftop and sampled each other for dessert. Ricky reserved the entire rooftop space so we could have some privacy, and we took advantage of our alone time in a Janet Jackson "Anytime, Anyplace" kind of way. Our waiter pretended not to see our wandering hands and lips, but his cheeks were rosy as hell and he was on half-chub when he brought us the check.

Ricky and I left walking hand in hand past a few paps who ate up the opportunity to snap pics of my peek-a-boo dress. Just as we were about to get in the car, a reporter from TMZ rushed over. He dapped up Ricky and told him that he loved his latest single. He then told me how amazing I looked and said he tried to get a bottle of LIT for his girlfriend, but it was sold out.

I didn't mind entertaining his random banter. That is until he asked, "Have you heard YB plans to make a record about you? Like a diss track?"

Ricky opened the door to our chauffeured SUV. "Let's go."

I chuckled, placed my shades on my face, and looked over my shoulder at the reporter. "Check my website for the perfume. Your girl will love it."

Before the guy could respond, I was in the backseat with Ricky sliding in beside me. After he closed the door in the pap's face, I waved at him from behind the tinted window. Ricky was on the phone with someone before we made it down the block.

"Aye, remember what we discussed… Yeah. Make sure everybody in the front knows… Nah, not really. Homie from TMZ just had somethin' to say, so that was my cue to touch base with you one last time… A'ight. We'll be there in about thirty minutes."

When he hung up, I rubbed his leg. "Babe, I hope you aren't pressed over YB's punk ass."

"I ain't pressed. I'm just tryin' to stay off papers."

"Okay, but you know we can't stop him from getting in the club."

"He's not gettin' into the spot where we'll be."

I snuggled next to him and smiled. Ricky is the realest man I've ever dealt with—from his promises to cause bodily harm to those who cross him to his unconditional love for me.

"You about to take a nap?" he asked as I rested my head against his arm.

I moaned my sound of affirmation and closed my eyes. After hearing him say on the phone we had a thirty-minute drive, it was lights out for me. All my people know I don't play about my power naps. My theory is you can't turn up if you haven't turned down first.

Ricky nudged me awake as we rode down a long, winding driveway.

"Where are we?" I asked, looking out the window.

As we got closer, a mansion came into view. It

wasn't an ordinary mansion. Whoever owned it came from old money. To the side, I saw what looked like a mini luxury car lot and a valet jogging back to his post in the circular driveway.

"Jazz called and said we should stop through this party he's hosting. If it's whack, we can just say 'What's up' and bounce," he answered.

I rolled my eyes and poured a shot of Ciroc. Jazz is the head of Ricky's record label and often invites us to his gatherings. He throws decent parties, but they are typically most appealing to new artists and groupies. I wanted to go shake somethin' at a club, not be around a bunch of fake-ass industry cats. I understood the game, though. Ricky had to make an appearance since we were in L.A. I was willing to take one for the team but only for an hour.

Once we stopped, I touched up my lipstick and shook my hair into place. "Will I know anybody here?"

"I don't see how you wouldn't," Ricky said after downing his glass of Crown.

"Maybe a better question would be, will I want to be bothered with them?"

He cut his eyes at me. "You ready?"

I nodded and he knocked on his window. Our driver, Melvin, opened the door, and Ricky stepped out. As I put on my shades and scooted toward his outstretched hand, I noticed there was a red carpet beneath his feet that led all the way to the mansion's entrance. The carpet was clear except for two women who were walking up the steps and nearing the entrance. They were too far away for me to see their faces. It looked like we had just missed the major arrivals, and I wasn't sure whether I was grateful for that or offended.

I barely had a leg out the door before a swarm of paparazzi ran over and nearly blinded me with the flashes from their cameras.

"Paris!"

"Paris, over here!"

"Work that dress, honey!"

"Can we get a view of the back?"

"You look amazing!"

"Ricky, can we get Paris by herself?" they called out.

*I guess we aren't that late*, I thought as I smoothed my dress down and posed for a few photos.

"Did you know it was gonna be this fancy?" I said in Ricky's ear when he got in the frame with me.

Maintaining my smile, I placed my hand on his chest, giving the photogs playful but sexy shots to pull from. Ricky ignored me and simply led me away from the cameras. We continued our trek toward the entrance, passing ice statues carved in the shape of flames and a large fountain that spewed reddish-orange water. Two hostesses greeted us with a choice of two specialty cocktails when we reached the steps. Careful not to mix light with dark, I chose Believe the Hype over Rowdy Brown.

I danced to the music on our way up to the double doors that made up the entrance. Ricky stopped me just before the last step.

"Hey," he started, "enjoy yourself tonight."

As long as I could have as many Believe the Hypes as my liver allowed, the odds of that happening were in my favor. He kissed me on my forehead, and the men guarding the doors opened them as if on cue. The foyer was crowded, but the first face I saw was my sister India's. Her smile spanned from one ear to the other.

"Happy Birthday!" she yelled along with the other guests.

I turned to Ricky.

"Surprise," he said with a wink.

"You did this?"

His smile was all the answer I needed. When I turned back to the crowd, I noticed Reign and KiKi standing next to India. Jordan was behind them. Most of the other faces belonged to my music industry peeps, athletes, actors, and old friends from school.

"Lyin' asses!" I said to Reign and KiKi, who both used the excuse of having to handle business in Atlanta as their reason for not being able to come to L.A. for my perfume launch the day before.

"We love you, too!" Reign replied as she hugged me.

"Shut up and dance!" KiKi added, hugging me and then leading me inside.

When I entered the dancehall, there were even more people...and stripper poles and a stage and a deejay booth with screens positioned on each side of it. A VIP area was roped off in the middle of the room. It allowed just enough space for a few people to sit on the couches, stand and mingle, or bust out a

F.I.R.E. dance routine. Ricky had the perfect setup for what he deemed my Thirty-Fly Celebration. The place reeked of adrenalin and good vibes; it gave me a high I didn't want to go away.

We'd been partying for over an hour when the music abruptly stopped. I was mid body roll.

Before I could question what happened, the deejay announced, "I heard it's time for some cake! Birthday girl, where you at?"

The spotlight forced me to squint. Once I was able to focus my eyesight again, I saw India rolling a cart onstage with a huge cake that was a replica of my perfume bottle. Jay-Z's "Young Forever" began playing, and images of me from birth to present day appeared on the screens. Ricky stood behind me with his arms wrapped around my waist. We swayed to the beat as I fought back tears.

When the slideshow ended, India lit the candles and Reign's distinct voice sounded through the speakers. "Happy Birthday to you…" She came into view as KiKi took over and joined her onstage. "Happy Birthday to you…" Instead of the two-part harmony I expected next, the voice I first heard in ninth grade during fourth period chorus sang the last "Happy Birthday…" laced with melodic runs.

Shai slowly walked out and joined Reign and KiKi. "…dear Paris."

Beneath her mink lashes were doe eyes that looked directly into mine. Nearly everyone in the space gasped when they saw Shai's face. My former groupmates finished with a three-part harmony that made me shudder as everyone cheered and screamed well wishes.

That broke me. I dabbed away tears, trying my best to preserve my makeup. My entire cool was gone, though. My baby had thrown me what was sure to be one of the most talked about parties of our era, and the chick I hadn't spoken to in three years surprised the hell out of me with a birthday serenade.

Ricky escorted me to the stage. The deejay handed me a mic before I headed over to the cake. I blew out all thirty-five candles in one breath.

"This doesn't mean I'm full of hot air like some of y'all say," I joked. "God just gave me high-capacity lungs. Pray for a set. Ask my husband why."

My sisters—biological and biographical—waited just a few feet away. India and I squeezed each other so tightly that we both lost our breath for a moment. There was no need for words. She knows how much I value my life after having almost lost it. Every year is now a big deal. Reign and I wrapped our arms around each other and rocked side to side. KiKi and I did our Birthday Bop dance that we came up with on my 21st birthday, and then we hugged. Shai wore an awkward smile when I turned toward her. We had to be thinking the same thing: how do you genuinely greet someone who was every variety of bitch you could and *did* name the last time you spoke? Our relationship hadn't hit a bump in the road. We didn't have a little spat. We had "Certified Angus" beef that has been slow-cooking since about 2005.

I'm allergic to being phony, but I once regarded her as one of my closest friends. Because I've known her since we were freshmen in high school, I was certain she had bubble guts, wondering if I was going to publicly shade her.

Shai held out her arms and raised her eyebrows slightly. "Surprise!"

For the first time in a long time, she didn't come off as pretentious or self-serving. She was humble and shy…and uncoached.

"Hell yeah, it's a surprise!" I replied, then walked over to accept her embrace. "Thanks for coming."

I tried to keep our hug short and sweet, but it turned into a minute-long hold with ugly cries. With my face nestled near her neck, I couldn't help but smell a familiar scent. She was wearing my fragrance.

# DISCONNECTED

**M**Y eyes popped open seconds before I heard the click of Colin's keycard unlocking our room door. His tardiness had become so routine that my body was programmed to wake just in time to hear his lies while they were fresh. Beneath my heavy, swollen lids, I watched him stroll in.

He pulled his t-shirt over his head while making his way to the bed. I peered at his chiseled, tattooed upper body, wondering who had been pressed against it. Before he slid off his pants, he took his phone out the pocket, powered it off, and placed it gently on the nightstand.

"Why even bother?" I asked, startling him a bit.

"What? Baby, go back to sleep. I didn't mean to wake you," Colin said.

I sat up slowly. "Just once, it would be nice if you didn't mean to keep me up all night waiting for you."

He threw his head back. "You kill me with that noise. You leave and go on tour for months, but I come in late a few times and you cry insomnia."

I pulled back the sheet and got out of bed. "What's funny about that is when I'm gone, it's because I'm working. When you're gone, it's because you're playing." I walked toward his side. "Be patient. At this rate, I'll be used to sleeping alone sooner than later. Five o'clock is a new record. You're training me well."

He shook his head and smiled. "Cute."

"Apparently not cute enough."

I retreated to the bathroom and let the hot shower water wash my tears away. Something had to give, and it couldn't be my sanity. Colin is the model husband when we have an audience. When we're alone, I never know what I'm getting. These days, I don't want it either way.

I hate to cry in front of him because he sees it as a sign of weakness. Really, I'm just frustrated. I've sacrificed a lot for him, only to get treated like I'm a basic chick who should be grateful he decided to marry me. I can think of a few thousand people who would love to be in his shoes. The problem is I don't want them. I've only wanted him. Until now.

No makeup, hair in a ponytail, hat pulled down low, earbuds in. I went to the hotel's fitness center to blow off some steam. Technically, I should have asked my bodyguard, Ian, to come along, but I wanted to be alone. Besides, it was early enough that I could slip in and out without encountering too many people.

I chose the elliptical machine that faced the corner. Though the workout center was empty, I anticipated the arrival of a few fitness enthusiasts at any moment and wanted to be as inconspicuous as possible. By the time they'd get there, I would probably be leaving, though. I only needed an hour—long enough for the endorphins to take over my body and remind me who I am.

It would be more accurate to say "who I'm told I am." My fans and the vast majority of anyone in the entertainment business will say I'm the best to ever do it—the prototype for female vocalists and entertainers, a bad bitch, etc. I made the cut for *People Magazine's* "50 Most Beautiful People" five times, sang at the White House, and had the pleasure of meeting the Queen of England.

I'm grateful for the life I've lived, but I guess for me, this is just what I do. For as long as I can remember, my mother had me in dance class and singing in the church choir. She taught me manners and etiquette and how to cook soul food like somebody's seventy-year-old grandmother. She paid for tutors to make sure I passed the classes I struggled in and told me that I needed to be well-rounded in case I was unable to secure a career in music. According to Uncle Zeke, though, I was born with this gift and my purpose is to bring others joy with the sound of my voice. Every year at Thanksgiving dinner, he tells everyone sitting around the table that he knew I was a star when I could barely talk but babbled the melody to Michael Jackson's "Thriller."

Let the world tell it, I'm living the dream and I'm every man's dream. Let me tell it, I question whether this was ever *my* dream. My mother never asked me what I aspired to be. She just assumed I was on board with her vision for me because I did what she told me to do. And though I genuinely fell for the man who is now a three-time NBA MVP, our courtship and marriage turned from an innocent boy-meets-girl situation to a media frenzy before we were sure what love is. Nevertheless, here we are eight years and two kids later living *somebody's* dream.

I was mouthing lyrics from Kendrick Lamar's latest album, when I heard the beeps of another machine. Someone else had arrived. I won't deny how great the breeze felt from the exercise bike's fan as the person pedaled behind me. It was a reciprocal cool-down to the one I was doing on the elliptical machine. Once I stopped, I stood still to let the air whip through my tank top.

The entry of an older gentleman startled me out of my trance. I wiped down the machine and then stopped at the cooler to gulp down two tiny cups of water. No sooner than my cup landed in the trashcan, a female voice called my name. She didn't sound sure that it was me, so I didn't turn to acknowledge her.

"BG!" she said louder.

Only three people called me that, and when I turned around, one of them was getting off the air bike. Reign and I went to high school together and, along with two other girls, we started F.I.R.E., the third bestselling R&B girl group of all time. I hadn't seen Reign in over a year, although we've had conversations about getting together numerous times. Out of all the girls, I kept in touch with her most consistently, so it was all love when I saw her smiling face.

Reign can light up any room. Her aura exudes love and peace. She's a calm soul. Even though we're in our thirties, there's still innocence in her eyes that explains how she succumbed to her vulnerabilities during our rise to the top.

She rushed over to me and we hugged. I apologized for being sweaty, but she waved me off.

"What are you doing in L.A.?" she asked.

"I came to support Colin," I replied. "He's speaking at a fundraiser for sickle cell tonight."

"Oh, okay! I saw Tionne tweeting about it," Reign said.

I leaned to get a view of her backside. "You look good!"

She covered her smile, but I could still see her rosy cheeks. "I'm trying. Squats do a booty good."

I joined in her laughter, but then seriously asked, "You've been doing it the right way this time, correct?"

41

I'd seen a few photos of Reign in the media, and her weight loss was evident. Although never obese, she was overweight in high school and instantly tagged "the big girl" of our group when we released our first single. It's one thing to be teased in school about your weight. It's a completely different monster when hundreds of thousands of people count how many rolls they see under your fitted shirts and go even further to say that evil crap right in front of you.

Reign nodded. "Kenz is a gym rat, so I go at least three times a week with her. I'm still on east coast time and couldn't sleep, so I brought my ass down here."

"Your *nice* ass!"

"Oww!" Reign twerked just long enough to get the old man's attention.

We laughed when we realized he'd seen her.

"You're looking snatched, as usual," Reign complimented.

"Stop it. I'm down here looking like a bum. How did you know it was me anyway? I never even looked your way."

She pointed to my left hand. "For one, you drum your fingers on the side of your thigh when you're nervous or upset about something. You've been doing it since I walked in."

I made a fist to stop the motion she referred to.

"Then I saw your tattoo fail as you were walking over to the water cooler," Reign continued.

When we were eighteen and nineteen, Reign, Paris, KiKi, and I went to get tattoos. Everybody left with colorful flames near their ankles except me. The artist attempted one line, and I cried like he was performing major surgery. I compromised to let him make one more line and left with a small "X".

"We don't have to go into details in the middle of this gym, but you have my number. I'm never inaccessible."

"I appreciate you, but I'm fine," I lied. "Just dealing with record label stuff."

"Okay. Well, we should catch up later anyway. I need to hear all about the little ones and whatever else you have going on, diva. In the meantime, I'm gonna get back to this cardio."

"Cool. We'll chat later."

Reign touched my shoulder and looked under my brim to make sure we made eye contact. "And when we do, you don't have to pretend you're okay."

I gave her a quick goodbye hug and blinked away a tear. Turned to walk away. Turned back around. "Hey, how's everybody else?" I blurted.

"Good. KiKi is filming for *Boss Ladies* the next two months and still being a ho."

I shook my head and giggled. KiKi has always loved attention from the fellas.

"Does she still talk to Jamal?"

"They talk and do whatever else they do," Reign replied.

There was an awkward silence that I finally broke. "And Paris?"

"Oh! Um, she's doing really well. You know about her perfume, right?"

"Of course. I don't think anyone could miss that news.

All I see are good reviews on the blogs and social media. I think it's cool she launched just before her birthday."

"Yeah. That's actually why I'm in town. KiKi's flying in this morning, too. Ricky's throwing a surprise party for Paris tonight, and he's goin' all out."

"That's sweet. Well, you guys have fun." My mouth formed what my uncle, Zeke, calls my public smile before I walked out.

As I exited the workout center, I felt worse than when I went in. I realized how disconnected I've been from the people who know me best. Reign hadn't seen me in forever but still treated me like her sister. She recognized me without seeing my face or hearing my voice. And after all I've done and haven't done, she still showed sincere concern for my emotional state. What hit me harder than anything was the fact she wasn't going to mention the other girls if I hadn't asked; and even after she told me what KiKi was up to, I had to prompt her for an update about Paris, the one I once had the closest relationship with.

There was definitely a rift in our friendship that was established right before F.I.R.E. broke up. Paris was on a path to destruction, and her recklessness was affecting all of us. She was late for appearances, wouldn't show up for rehearsals, and had random outbursts during interviews. I'd say much of that was attributed to her love for Mary Jane (weed) and Brandon (YB). There's no denying she was rightfully and lovingly known as the party girl of the group, but when she turned twenty-one, life turned her out.

Our last conversation wasn't pretty. It took place three years ago, a couple weeks after her wedding. She was pissed because I didn't feel like singing with her and the girls per the guests' requests. There was no pressing reason. I was just PMS'ing and didn't feel like being bothered for the sake of giving a few people their nostalgic fix. I think Paris would've gotten over it fairly quickly if she hadn't seen footage of me singing "Endless Love" at Nico Moretti's wedding a week later…with YB.

Nico sprung the last-minute request on me after I cancelled an appearance in the Bahamas thanks to a hurricane. YB was still Public Enemy #1 in Paris' eyes, so I told Nico I'd be honored to sing but preferably not with YB. Zeke jumped in and said I would do it, later scolding me in private for being unprofessional. He reminded me not to let personal issues play a part in my business decisions and asked if I thought Paris was turning down money from anyone based on my feelings. He also reminded me that even though I wasn't getting a check, Nico is the president of NV Records, the company I'm signed to, and would always remember his wife crying while I belted out the lyrics to her favorite song on their special day. That memory could come in handy when it came time to renegotiate my contract.

I meant to reach out to Paris before it took place, but time got away from me. The next thing I knew, Paris showed up at my house, phone in hand, with YouTube footage of the wedding playing. When I tried to explain that I told Nico I preferred not to sing with YB, she wasn't hearing it. When I told her how Zeke interfered and said "yes" for me, she accused me of having no backbone. In her mind, I should have said, "No." Period. Her exact words were, "I know English was your weakest subject, but 'No' is a complete sentence. Try it one day."

I was a "raggedy bitch," "low down," a "bum bitch," "traitor"—everything but a child of God. She said nasty, unfounded things about those closest to me: my mom sucked record execs off so I could get a solo deal, my husband is gay, and my uncle is a sleazy child molester. She wanted to hurt me, and she succeeded. Hurt people hurt people.

All these years, I've attributed her rant to the Patrón I smelled on her breath and the self-esteem issues she was dealing with at the time. I figured we were both busy living life and just hadn't taken the time to reach out and officially squash the drama from that day. Besides, we're both stubborn, too. I had been confident that if we saw each other at an event, we'd be cordial. How could we not? She'd never bashed me in interviews; and I'd seen her multiple times on TV and social media congratulating me on my latest projects and urging people to support.

But, Reign wasn't going to mention her to me. She purposely spoke only of KiKi. Now I'm thinking Paris is still holding on to that moment I let go after she sped away from my property. I've been so wrapped up in my life that in the past three years, I never picked up the phone to so much as text any of the women I once shared so much of my life with. Any communication I had with Reign and KiKi was initiated by them. So, I have no right to feel left out when I give no indication of wanting to be included.

Zeke sat across from me and watched as I took a bite of my Philly Cheesesteak Dog. I couldn't come to town without linking up with him. "I should take a picture and send it to Onyx," he said with his face scrunched.

"Snitch," I replied, my mouth still full.

Onyx is my personal trainer, and if he'd known I was at Pink's devouring my favorite hot dog like it was my last meal, he would have passed out. I didn't care. My people know I'm an emotional eater, and at twelve noon, I was an emotional disaster. Zeke was lucky I didn't order fries, too. It was his fault we were there anyway, "Mr. It's Good for the Fans to See You Doing Regular Things." I wasn't sure how regular it was to have my bodyguard sitting at the next table ready to jump on anyone who confused fandom with psychosis, but it was what it was.

"I'm trying to get you in at Children's Hospital while you're here. Remember that guy who was shot and killed like two weeks ago 'cause the cops thought he was breaking into his own house?" Zeke asked.

I nodded.

47

"His three-year-old daughter is in the cancer unit."

"Oh, no! Cancer?"

"Yep. They found out a couple days ago. Just imagine what type of press you'll get if you go see her. You're here until next week, right?"

I was done ingesting my food, but it took a moment for me to digest what Zeke said and how he said it. "Wait. How did her illness turn into my press coverage?"

Zeke laughed and waved me off. "Stop being so sensitive. You know there will be press there if you go. I'm just saying this is one of the biggest news stories out right now. The timing is perfect."

I felt sick to my stomach. Zeke used to be a genuine guy, but as F.I.R.E.'s success grew, so did his ego. And when I went solo, he only got worse. His intentions are driven solely by money now instead of my best interest, though he feels like he's looking out for me.

"I was supposed to stay until Wednesday, but I'm probably heading out Sunday," I told him.

"Sunday? That's in two days! I can't get you in before then."

"Sorry. I'd love to go visit her, but I'm ready to get back to my babies."

My text alert went off, prompting me to look at my phone. The message was from Reign.

> **Reign:** Hey, luv. It was great seeing u earlier. Really want u to come to Paris' party tonight if ur free. Cleared it with Ricky. Need u there at 8. Let me know.

I set my phone on the table and pretended to listen to Zeke's PR lecture. Meanwhile, my mind was on whether I would attend Paris' birthday party. I wanted to believe she couldn't hate me if Reign felt comfortable inviting me, but since Reign is a peacemaker at heart and often thinks optimistically rather than realistically, I struggled with making an informed decision.

"I'll stay until Monday night," I said to Zeke. "If you can't make it happen before five, I'll just have to send a few gifts instead."

"Yeah, yeah. Is Colin going back with you?"

"I don't know what he's doing, and I don't care," I muttered.

"Here we go with this again. What happened?"

"The usual, except he had the nerve to stroll in at five this time."

Zeke gave me his speech about letting men be men and how I of all people should know how challenging it has to be for him to balance the roles of family man and a handsome, athletic phenom. I've heard some shocking things from my uncle over the years, but that statement definitely earned a spot in the top three.

I'm very aware that I'm no troll. Back when I was younger, I used to get beat up because girls thought I was pretty and tried to bash my face in. And as a Grammy award-winning, platinum-selling artist, I'm a phenom myself. That doesn't entitle me to come and go as I please and act like a single woman, though. It was insulting for Zeke to come at me like I should excuse Colin's behavior for the sake of my image.

That's what it boiled down to. Whenever Colin and I get into our ugliest of arguments, Zeke is the one who sends me flowers with thoughtful apologies on the card. He doesn't know I know, but he once had the site up on his computer when I stopped by unexpectedly. Part of a message was typed in the text box. When I got home a few hours later, the flowers arrived along with the entire message printed on the card…*With love, from Colin.*

Zeke is hell-bent on making sure Colin and I keep up the façade that we are living in marital bliss with our two perfect children, multiple houses, and lucrative careers. It's apparently good for business. He's always found a way to tell me that without coming right out and saying it.

"What time is the event tonight?" Zeke asked.

"Seven." I wiped my mouth and fingers before picking up my phone to text Reign back.

**Me:** What's the address?

"Babe, can you help me with this bowtie?"

I exited the bathroom and found Colin standing in front of the mirror, struggling. As usual, he looked handsome in his tuxedo. I pointed to the bed and he sat down to allow me access. At 5'6", it's laughable for me to attempt to reach the neck attached to his 6'7" stature.

Once I finished, he rested his hands on my hips and stared at me for a few seconds. I diverted my eyes

50

before asking what he was looking at.

"We good?"

We'd spent some time in the room together before we both got dressed, but we barely spoke. Our faces were glued to our devices in an effort to ignore the elephant in the room. Colin's question was his version of caring about my feelings. Never mind that he continues to hurt them in the first place.

I leaned down and kissed his forehead before stepping back. "You're all set," I told him, straightening his bowtie.

"Wait. Why do you have that on?" he asked.

The event was a black-tie affair. I had on romper with a V-neck that reached my belly button.

"Because this is what I'm wearing tonight."

"Babe, do you remember what type of event this is? I mean, you look damn good, but you can't go like that."

"I know," I said as I walked back to the bathroom to finish applying my makeup.

"Shai, do you know how it would look if you showed up like that? It'll kill your image. Mine, too."

"I know."

He came around the corner holding the garment bag that housed my ball gown. "Here."

I finished lining one eyelid before turning to him. "You can hang it on the door. I don't need it. For once, I'm not concerned about our image."

"Have you been drinking or something? What's up with you? You know you're not going with me dressed like that, right?"

I set my eyeliner on the counter and exhaled audibly. "Colin, I'm not going with you tonight. I have another engagement."

"What engagement?"

"One with people who care more about my feelings than you. You don't need me around, baby. You'll do great." Back to my makeup.

Colin laughed with disbelief. "I don't know what women's empowerment conference you went to this afternoon, but I don't have time for this shit. The car will be here in an hour."

"And mine will be here in fifteen minutes. So, excuse me." I brushed past him and organized my purse. Before putting my phone inside, I texted Ian to let him know I was ready.

"Shai, you're really not going? What am I supposed to tell people?"

"You're good at lying. Tell them whatever you want. My answer is no."

"What up, Superstar!" KiKi said when I walked in.

Reign had met me at the back door and escorted me to a room with a piano where KiKi was playing a melody.

"Stop," I said.

She got up from the bench and gave me a quick hug. "To what do we owe the pleasure?"

In an effort to keep things cordial, I entertained her with an answer. "I'm not sure what you mean. I'm here to celebrate Paris' birthday like everyone else."

"After missing the past what, eight? Cool. Welcome."

"Wh— "

"Alright! Let's rehearse and make sure our harmonies are in tune. Shall we?" Reign interjected.

Her face beamed with excitement as she shared her vision for the night. Since her lower register is unmatched, she would start off our rendition of "Happy Birthday." KiKi was to go next, and then I would go last. She wanted us to come out separately, making my attendance even more of a surprise.

Suddenly, my stomach was in knots. What if Paris didn't want to see me? I'd let my annoyance with Colin drive my RSVP, and there I was just an hour away from coming face to face with the woman who just had a public outburst regarding someone who she's not on good terms with. I didn't want to trend on Twitter because she embarrassed me at her party. It was too late for all that thinking, though. I was already in the building and couldn't think of an excuse to leave that wouldn't jinx a member of my family.

When we practiced, our voices blended like we had rehearsed for days. Once we worked out a few kinks, we were extra hype. I'd forgotten how fun it was to share moments of vocal brilliance with someone else until we hit that perfect three-part harmony at the end of the song and started high-fiving each other and screaming out, "Yes!"

We finished up minutes before the deejay filled the

place with the sounds of the hottest music from the past and present. KiKi and I attempted to catch up while Reign stepped away to help with an issue at the door. I congratulated her on being picked up for a third season on *Boss Ladies*, and I asked if she'd been working on new music for herself.

"Nah," she replied. "I know how to recognize when my time has passed. I make plenty of money staying behind the scenes."

"Well, if that's the case, I wouldn't mind you writing some stuff for me!" I told her.

"Stop frontin', Shai. It's enough that you showed up to the party. Doing extra isn't required."

"What's that supposed to mean?"

"Man, I sent songs to you and Zeke years ago—songs other artists recorded and ended up winning Grammys for. I don't need you to try to enhance my self-esteem or whatever it is you think you're doing. I'm good."

"Sent songs to *me*? Via what?"

She clarified that she'd sent them directly to Zeke and said he responded every time with, *These are great, but this is not the direction we're going in. Shai sends her thanks and well wishes.*

"On everything, I never knew of this. I wish you would have contacted me directly."

"Why? So you could 'New phone, who 'dis?' me again? Or so I could hear the number was no longer in service? Nah, Shai. You know I don't roll like that. You make sure you add important people to your contacts or you let those people know when your contact info changes. You got me twice with that shit. I'm not that important to you, and it's okay."

I didn't know what to say. I was guilty of not keeping in touch with many people, but I often depended on my assistant to handle phone contacts as part of her administrative duties. The bad part about that is she determined who was important and who wasn't. The worse part about that is I never noticed my former group members weren't added until I saw them in person.

My text alert went off. Since my phone was on the table in front of us, KiKi saw it was Colin. I picked up the phone so I could read.

"I assume he's coming?" KiKi asked.

> **Colin:** Really wish u were here. I looked stupid walking the carpet alone n everybody's asking about u. Where r u?

"No. He's attending another event tonight," I answered while also replying to Colin.

> **Me:** Tell them I'm at a birthday party. If you run into Tionne, tell her I said hey.

KiKi twisted her lips and nodded her head. It was always awkward when we talked about Colin because she dated him briefly before I did and has been especially peeved because we ended up marrying and starting a family.

"How are the babies?" she asked.

"Good. You know CJ turns eight in a couple months."

"Yeah, I know. I can't believe he's that old now! And

Journey will be eight in August," she added, referring to Reign's daughter.

"You still don't want any?"

"No, nope, and nah."

Her reply caused us both to laugh.

Reign rushed into the room to tell us Paris had arrived and was walking the carpet. She summoned KiKi to join her at the front door so they could be a part of the initial surprise but instructed me to wait in the room. For at least an hour, I entertained myself by scrolling through Instagram, taking selfies, and couch-dancing to the music. When we had about ten minutes left before we hit the stage, I made my way to the bathroom because...bubble guts.

We stood behind the stage while Paris' slideshow played. I gulped down the remainder of my Believe the Hype cocktail and took a deep breath. Reign grabbed my hand, stopping my fingers from tapping my thigh. She reached out for KiKi's hand, too. We huddled in order to hear her.

"Ladies, let's enjoy this moment and focus on celebrating our sister on her special day—nothing else. I want both of you to know that I love you, and nothing could ever change that. I could not have made this happen without either of you."

She squeezed my hand and winked at me before mouthing, *It's okay.*

To my surprise, it was. Paris didn't mask her emotions when I walked onstage. Our eyes met while I sang to her, and I was relieved to see her mouth open with shock rather than twisted in disgust.

After she blew out her candles and hugged her sister, Reign, and KiKi, I opened my arms and blurted a barely audible, "Surprise!"

"Hell yeah, it's a surprise!" Paris said, accepting my gesture.

Instantly, tears fell—crocodile tears—accompanied with sobs I was glad the audience couldn't hear. Paris was crying, too. There was no single reason why I was so emotional, and I surely didn't expect to bawl in front of hundreds of people recording us on their phones. But, it happened, and I didn't care.

Reign and KiKi wrapped their arms around us for a group hug and walked us offstage while the deejay got the party going again. In the hallway, Paris gushed over how great we sounded and how the night had been amazing. She barely formed complete sentences as her mouth tried to keep up with the thousands of thoughts swirling around in her brain.

We all decided to link up again as soon as the party ended so she could get back to entertaining her guests. Besides, the Migos had just slipped past us and were about to perform "Bad and Boujee" for her.

Before Paris walked away, she pulled me aside. "Is that my perfume?"

I winked. "I asked my assistant to grab one from your in-store yesterday."

# NO LOVE

**J**AMAL raised my leg and slid inside of me. I welcomed him with a whimper and closed my eyes. He is the only man who has ever made me feel the tingles most women speak of when they describe their sexual encounters. Some of the other guys I've had sex with were amazing, but they didn't give me the bonus feelings Jamal's magic stick came with.

Paris told me it's because we make love. I don't doubt she knows what she's talking about, but I don't love Jamal—not like that. I've been close with Jamal for years. He went to Whittaker High School with us and was in my graduating class. We became close once he learned I could flow. So, we kicked it all the time and would come up with rhymes together in his room. To this day, we're best friends, and that's the only love I have for him.

I struggle with that word. I've seen too many people throw "love" around recklessly, hurting the very people they claim to adore. So, I've avoided living the fairytale life of boy meets girl, boy and girl get married, and boy and girl live happily ever after. It really goes like this: boy meets girl, boy and girl get married, boy meets other girls, boy acts like he's not married, wife-girl finds out, but boy and wife-girl post pictures of themselves hugged up on social media like they're happy. I prefer to save my acting skills for the big screen and getting poor-performance dudes out of my vagina.

My ongoing rebuttal to Paris' explanation is that Jamal and I have a natural chemistry that stems from our longtime friendship. That's it. Besides, he has a girlfriend, and I have my low-Ki's. So, we just do what we do and go about our days like nothing happened. Some people hug when they're happy to see each other. We have sex.

"Damn, I missed this," he groaned near my ear.

His strokes became stronger. I gripped the nearby towel ring for leverage.

"How much?" I asked, throwing it right back.

Five minutes later, it was evident just how much. I snatched the towel from the towel ring and stuffed part of it in his mouth to muffle his moans. I was pretty sure the walls weren't thick enough to keep Dawn from hearing us.

After we took a moment to recover, he pointed at the mirror and laughed. "That yoga class is producing results."

"I know, right? Wipe that shit off!"

I've always been flexible because my parents made me take dance classes for ten years, but yoga took that flexibility to another level. I could mess around and be a contortionist these days. Jamal and I snickered as he took a towel to the mirror and wiped away the prints from the tips of my toes.

He washed up at the sink as I turned on the water for my shower.

"You think Paris knows?" he asked.

"About tonight? Nah. I've been throwing her off, sending updates about the party she thinks she's having back home. She has no idea."

"That's what's up. Well, Dawn will be excited to see it all go down. You already know she loves y'all."

"She wouldn't love *me* if she knew we were fucking in the hotel room next to hers."

"You never know," he replied with a smirk.

I rolled my eyes.

"There you go," he said. "What?"

"You know *what*. She's subpar. You need to let that go. Been telling you that for what, six years now?" I started singing the hook of Drake's song, "Marvin's Room."

He dried off and pulled on his underwear. "Well, everybody ain't you, and since you ain't tryna be my girl…"

"Boy, stop. You've been bonin' me the whole time you've been with her. IF I wanted a relationship, do you really think I would consider being with you so you can do the same thing to me? You don't want those problems, and you know it, sir. You'd be the next *Dateline* murder mystery."

"Nah. If I had the prototype, there's nothing an imitator could do for me. Have you ever wondered why I keep coming back for more? And why you keep giving it to me?" he asked before delivering a smack to my bare ass and kissing me on the cheek. "I'll see you tonight."

I smiled and got in the shower. I knew why he kept coming back. They all come back. But, I did wonder why I kept giving it to him. There's only one other man I'd consistently had sex with in all my years of intercoursing. That was Colin, and we were in a relationship then.

My time in the shower was cut short when my phone rang back to back. Knowing the ringtone was personalized for my mother, I hurriedly wrapped myself in a towel and answered her fourth call.

"You'll never guess who just called here," she said.

"You're probably right. Who?" I asked.

My mother is the queen of hyping up stuff that only excites her.

"Your father."

I slowly lowered myself onto the toilet seat. I grew up thinking my stepfather was my biological father until they divorced. His new wife, who was jealous of our relationship, broke the news to me. I was sixteen. When I asked my mother who my real father was, she told me that he was some dude she'd had a one night stand with. She only knew his first name, what he looked like at age twenty-three, his sponsor family's phone number, and that he was in the United States on a student visa, attending MIT for architecture. She said they met at a party while she was visiting our family in Boston. It was her last night in town, and she spoke with him twice after that over the phone. Six weeks later, a doctor told her that I was growing inside of her. He was back home in Venezuela, and she never spoke to him again.

On my twentieth birthday, I decided I would look for him. I guess my search was prompted by the thought of my mother being that age and learning she would have to raise me alone. Since I had more money and resources than she did when she first tried to find him, I just knew I'd be successful. That wasn't the case, though. After two years of false leads, imposters, and dead-end searches, I decided to let it go. I walked away with his full name, old addresses, disconnected phone numbers, and a broken heart. It took a while, but I grew comfortable knowing I'd never have a relationship with my real dad.

"My father?" I asked. "Joe?"

Though I knew she probably wasn't talking about my stepfather, I wanted to clarify.

"No, baby. Daniel. We finally found him."

Unbeknownst to me, she had the private

investigators start their search again after I told her that I have no desire to settle down, get married, and have children. I knew it concerned her. She thinks my feelings about men stem from never knowing my father, but I didn't think she'd ever go that far. Besides, what would a relationship with him change when I'm a grown-ass woman in my thirties? Regardless, the investigators had found success after one more year of searching for Daniel Herrera—the curly-haired man with the thick accent who, in only a few hours, stole my mother's heart and her uterus back in 1980.

"He wants to see you," she continued. "He lives in Vancouver, but he said he's willing to travel wherever. He asked for your number, but I didn't want him to call and catch you off guard."

"Like you just did?"

I know she meant well, but I was aggravated. You don't drop heavy shit on someone without a lead-in, and you certainly don't do it when they have to keep up a certain persona in front of hundreds of people within hours. What was I supposed to do with that information? How was I supposed to feel?

I didn't have time to process it. I told my mother we would talk about it when I returned to Atlanta the next day. In the meantime, I needed to take a couple shots and get dressed for Paris' party.

I told Paris and Reign she was bad news. From the moment Shai stepped in the front office with her mother to enroll, I knew it. Sophomore year, I was an office aide during second period. So, I saw a lot of people come and go and heard a lot of inside scoop about incoming students. I didn't hear much about Shai—just that she'd moved around a lot because of her mother's job and had come to Whittaker High from some school in Birmingham, Alabama. But, something told me there was more to it, like she was running away from something.

Back then, I couldn't explain it beyond saying she looked like a victim or a fake. The resident-vacant look in her eyes prevented me from believing anything about her was authentic. The girls laughed at me when I told them, and I can see how it probably sounded ridiculous. But, that was the only verbiage I could come up with. Why? Because my opinion of her was formed mostly from an inkling, and it's hard to make others feel what's in your gut. So, I looked like a hater. Paris even accused me of being jealous because a lot of people said Shai and I looked alike, only she was more girly. I guess I was supposed to feel some type of way, but nah. I was comfortable with myself. She was a pretty girl, so I wasn't insulted. I just didn't trust her ass.

They believe me now, though. They believed me

when she put us on blast during our *Teen Summit* appearance in 1999, telling the audience she was the only one who was still a virgin. They believed me when she started dating Colin months after he and I broke up. And when she looked us in our faces and revealed she'd been working on a solo album behind our backs, I didn't hold back the I-told-you-so's.

Shai is the queen of, "What? Huh? I never meant any harm." Her greatest talent is playing dumb. Until her seat is adequately warmed in hell, I have several reserved for her on God's green Earth.

Language Arts was never her strong point, but that chick is calculating as hell. If math or statistics are involved, she's on some *Hidden Figures* type-a-shit. She's analytical. She understands perception, and cause-and-effect, and how that affects her money. That's why she's hugely successful. That's why she agreed to come to Paris' party.

When Reign told me that she invited Shai, I almost shook her. She wants to believe everyone is a good person at their core, and that often gets her (and the rest of us) in trouble. I questioned why Shai wanted to come when she hadn't so much as texted Paris in years.

It felt like a publicity stunt to me. Paris was back in the spotlight with her new perfume; her comment about the song with YB had Black Twitter on fire; and she was about to be on the cover of *Essence*. God forbid Paris get some shine while Shai's taking time away from the stage to focus on her family. Nope. She couldn't let that happen. Since she didn't have an album to drop overnight, attending Paris' party would do. She specialized in stepping on Paris' toes whenever she could; and to be fair, Paris used to do the same to her, too.

I hadn't spoken to Shai since we ran into each other at the BMI Awards a year prior. We hugged and posed for the cameras, caught up for a moment, and moved along. That's what our "friendship" has consisted of since she left the group. We're cordial passers-by. So, when we came face to face alone in the piano room, the vibe was awkward.

"I'm guessing the camera crew out in the hallway is with you for *Boss Ladies*?" she asked when Reign left us alone.

I nodded. "First month of filming. I told them they could only roll during the party."

"I love it. Congrats on another season!"

I thanked her, then she went on and on about how courageous one has to be to sign up for reality TV.

"It can be a bad move for some," I replied. "I'm an open book, so it doesn't intimidate me. The people whose relationships and careers get destroyed are the ones who try to present their fake lives as real."

"What's up on the music side? Are you going to do another album? The industry could use some bars from KiKi."

I couldn't help but smile at her nod to my capabilities as an MC, but I explained that I'm a behind-the-scenes girl now. I make great money writing and producing for other artists. The solo album I put out years ago when F.I.R.E. was still going strong only went gold. That's an accomplishment but not anything to write home about. I'd be silly to think a new album from me would do any better after we've been apart for almost ten years. When I feel the itch to be heard, I simply do a collab with another artist.

She almost ruined the vibe when she said I could write some songs for her. It came off like she was throwing me a bone or just saying it because it sounded good for the moment. I sent at least twenty songs to Zeke for her over a few years. This was after I got over her leaving the group and came out of my depression-laden, drunken stupor. Since life had handed me a basket full of lemons, I decided to stop squeezing them into my tequila and make lemonade, lemon meringue pie, lemon muffins—*anything*—instead.

I had written some of my dopest ballads while dealing with F.I.R.E.'s breakup, and the world needed to hear them. At that point, I didn't care who sang them. I just wanted a fair publishing agreement and writing credit. In a perfect world, I would've been the artist. But, in a more profitable world, Shai could sing my songs and I would ride her double-platinum wave to the bank. Her first album had been a huge success, and so I figured I could still get my coins with her—just in a different way. Truth be told, she owed me that.

The last time I presented my music to Zeke was in 2009. I actually met with him in person. We were on our fourth track, and he was bobbing his head, clearly vibing with the music. The song, "For Real This

Time," was my favorite of the five I had recorded for him to hear. When it was time for the bridge, I sang along, executing one of the baddest runs I've ever done. I smiled at Zeke, knowing I killed it, and before the chorus came in again, he stopped the music.

As he hopped from his chair, he hit me with, "I applaud your efforts, Jakirah. I'm proud of you. This isn't the direction Shai is going in, though. It's too R&B. We want more of a pop feel. Keep working hard and call my people when you have more."

Mind you, two of the songs were of pop appeal.

I was beyond livid. He spoke to me like I was a seventh grader who just learned to play the piano and sucked at it. *Call his people?* I had never called his people. I called him. And I didn't need him to be proud of me. A pat on the back wasn't gonna feed me. I was especially pissed because Shai's first single from her second album was a fucking R&B song.

Today, I can laugh about it. I can thank Zeke. Because they turned the songs down, I had to go out of my comfort zone and shop my music to artists who weren't in my circle. I sold "For Real This Time" to Kenya, who sang her face off, attained double-platinum status, and won a Grammy. Since then, I've written six other songs for her and many more for other artists.

Ironically, Kenya used to be an enemy of F.I.R.E. She was a background singer for Ashanti, who was on tour with us, and that broad was obnoxious. Kenya would make a point to sing our songs when she was

71

around us, doing #teamtoomuch runs and remixing shit. She was insinuating that she was a better vocalist than any of us and had made snide remarks about real talent being overlooked in the industry simply because of skin color. Kenya is dark-skinned and was convinced that's why she hadn't been signed as a lead vocalist. Never mind her stank-ass attitude.

She was like an obnoxious five-year-old, determined to get our attention even if it was negative. She boned one of our bodyguards (which got him fired). She offered Zeke oral sex, thinking he would get her a deal. And in a couple cities, we had issues with our microphones, even though soundcheck was incident-free. Shit hit the fan when she offered Reign a peace offering and we learned it was a case of SlimFast. Paris and I found her, locked her in a backstage bathroom, and held her down while we forced her to drink the French Vanilla flavored shake. She only made it through half of the case before puking all over herself. That was the end of our problems with her.

I believed Shai when she told me that she didn't know Zeke had listened to my music. He's such a snake, but of course, she's never acknowledged it because he's her uncle. I guess she's never had to, though, because he always makes sure she's straight. There's no reason to question someone's managerial skills when your money is right, your PR & marketing teams consist of geniuses, and your music transcends racial and cultural barriers. I can see how she could be blind to the truth.

When it comes to Colin, though, not so much. I peeped his game after four months of being with him. He's the great pretender, more concerned about what everyone else thinks about him than who he really is. I tried to warn Shai about him, but she thought I was jealous of their happiness and trying to come between them since I had dated him before.

Nope! I was worried about *her* happiness. But, once that heifer told me I should be more concerned with why I pushed him away and into someone else's arms, my concern expired. They've been married now for years and have the cutest kids, but I wonder how many of her nights are spent alone and if she knows who he's spending his nights with. I'm sure she doesn't. But, when the truth comes out, I'll have some hit songs about lies, deception, and heartbreak ready for her to record.

I dared one blogger to report that we didn't sing flawlessly on that stage. Three-fourths of F.I.R.E. reunited to sing to our groupmate, and we killed that shit. I browsed social media as I waited at the airport, just to see what the buzz was. As I expected, rumors swirled that we were in talks of reuniting for real this time. It was true. We'd agreed to check our schedules and arrange a meeting to discuss the possibility of resurrecting our group. Our long-time fans never stopped loving us, and we had even acquired a younger demographic who appreciate our presence on Instagram and Snapchat. For me, it was a no-brainer. We needed to put our differences aside and release one more album. And since the real money is in touring, we needed to make that happen, too. We pretended to be cohesive for the last two or three years of our career before. We could do it again. How hard would it be to put on our public smiles, perform like professionals, and go home for one more year?

I posted a snap of me at the airport with my hood and sunglasses on. Captioned it, "The Aftermath." I don't know what possessed me to take a nine a.m. flight home after partying all night. I could still taste weed and Rowdy Brown on my breath, even though I'd brushed my teeth and was chewing gum. What a night! L.A. didn't owe me a thing.

I lined up with the first-class group and leaned against the wall for support. Still on Snapchat, I viewed my cousin's story and then Paris'. I saw Dawn had posted, too. So, I opened hers to see what she had captured from Paris' party. She had footage of the strippers hanging upside down on the pole, bottles of champagne being popped, her dancing with Jamal, Paris twerking, and us singing. She even snagged a pic with Ricky and Paris. Her last photo caused me to swallow my gum. It was a picture of her wearing a diamond ring. The caption read, "Best night ever. I said yes! Duh!"

Reign!

# LOVE REIGNS

**M**ickie and I agreed to meet in the facility's parking lot at ten minutes 'til eight. Our mother was scheduled to be released from Twin Lakes Recovery Center at nine. She'd been there ninety days and had become unrecognizable—in a good way—the last time we visited.

We'd been down this road before with her. I remember when she would be gone for weeks at a time when we were little, and our family friend, Leanne, would take care of us while she was "away doing a few shows." By the time I turned twelve, I figured out it was all a lie. Summer had left rehab prematurely, and the night she'd come home from her "tour," I watched her convulse and writhe all over our kitchen floor, going through withdrawal. We had just finished the drug abuse unit in health class, so I knew exactly what I was witnessing.

The few months after that were hellish for both of us. I had a million questions, and Summer didn't want to provide one answer. I persisted because I deserved answers—all of them. I wanted to know how long she had been on drugs, what drugs she used, why she used them, and why she couldn't or wouldn't stop using them. Finally, I solicited Leanne's help, and my mother sat down and told me the truth. That day, I learned you have to be careful what you ask for. It was the day I learned I was a "crack baby" and that my attention issues and learning disability were not my fault.

Summer is a true hippie from Billings, Montana. She proudly proclaims she was born a rebel. That means she rebelled against her parents, teachers, the law, and sometimes herself. Though she may have been a handful, she was naturally gifted, and my grandparents made sure they exposed her to all the things she was interested in. Because of that, she plays piano, guitar, drums, and the violin; she sews clothing without a pattern; she is amazing at oil painting; and she speaks four languages fluently. Oh, and she's an eight-time Grammy Award-winning artist who received their Lifetime Achievement Award a few years ago.

My mother was in the music business for twenty-three years and was a godsend for F.I.R.E. when we signed our first contracts. The lawyer Shai's mother knew from their church didn't pick up on several clauses that would have made us slaves to the label and Zeke. Luckily, Summer was coherent that day and eloquently pointed out how one-sided the contract was, using her experience in the music business as well as the knowledge she obtained during her one year of law school. She flat-out told the execs that I wasn't even allowed to pick up the pen until they got their legal team in the room and made changes. Since the other girls' parents trusted her, they refused to sign, too. We are all still grateful for her. If Summer hadn't been there with us, we would still owe Hypeman Records a few albums and a lot of money.

"Oh, I meant to tell you she can only stay with me for a couple nights," Mickie said as we walked into the main building.

"What? I thought you said you'd keep your eye on her for a week," I replied, stopping in my tracks.

"Why can't she stay with you for the other days?"

"Because I'm going to L.A. You knew that, Mickie."

"Is your girlfriend going, too? She can't be at the house with her? I thought you two are such a loving family. She shouldn't mind."

He knew good and well I didn't like our mother at my house unless I was there. And even if that wasn't the case, no, Mackenzie was not in town. My nanny, Ms. Violet, was going to be at the house with Journey. Mickie was just being difficult. And, of course, he had to mention Mackenzie because he's still salty that his teenage celebrity crush is a lesbian and sleeping with his big sister.

79

"You are unbelievable," I replied. "If Kenz and I could accommodate her, we would be happy to, but that's unfortunately not an option at the time. I guess I have to figure it out, though, as usual."

He shrugged as we approached the front desk.

"Femi Adel and Michelob Fisher here to pick up Summer Grace."

I said Mickie's full name purposely, knowing it would piss him off. I could feel him glaring at me but kept my attention on the receptionist.

We waited in silence for about thirty minutes. During that time, I texted back and forth with Ricky about Paris' surprise party. He told me that he decided to do a slideshow for her and wanted my opinion on whether to show it before or after we sang "Happy Birthday" to her. He also needed some candid photos from our early F.I.R.E. days to include. One stood out in my mind: the four of us standing with Summer, holding our signed contracts and cheesing super hard.

I also had time to make arrangements for an aide to go to Summer's house to keep an eye on her on the days Mickie said she couldn't stay at his place. Though I was annoyed he was backing out of his responsibilities and placing them on me, it was probably for the best. Mickie is thirty-three but acts like he's twenty-three more often than not. Having a trained aide with our mother would give me peace of mind while I was away.

When I heard someone humming the melody to "Caged Bird," I immediately looked up and saw

Summer walking toward us with her rolling suitcase.

"Don't let me get free. You will never catch me," I sang along. I still remember being in the studio with her when she recorded it. "You look good, M—, Summer."

I walked over and hugged her tightly.

"No. You were right the first time. It's okay." She winked. "Call me Mom. That's who I am to you, right? At least it's who I'm supposed to be."

She could tell I was taken by surprise. In my thirty-five years on this earth, she'd insisted on me calling her by her first name. It was weird, especially when I didn't hear any other kids calling their parents by their first names. But, she always reassured me by saying their parents weren't as cool as her. I prayed that with the new name came new behavior.

"Mickie McTrouble!" she called out.

Mickie hugged her and kissed her on the cheek.

"No offense, but I hope I never see any of you again. I'm too old for this shit," Mom called out to the staff members.

"Well, we hope we don't see you again either, Summer," the middle-aged nurse said. "But, it was our pleasure having you."

When we made it to our cars, I hugged my mother again and told her I'd call her that evening. She seemed disappointed that I wouldn't be going to Mickie's house to get her settled. I reminded her that I had to catch my flight to L.A.

"Oh, that's right! Tell my baby, Paris, that I love her. Is she still with that chunky guy?"

"She's *married* to Ricky, Mom. And why does he have to be the chunky guy?"

"Hell! I don't know! I don't stock his refrigerator."

Her comment reminded me of the ones she made when I struggled with my weight, and I wasn't trying to be in that mental space again. "Okay. I gotta go. Love you. Behave yourself. I'll see you in a few days."

"Okay. When you come back, I need you to book me some studio time. I wrote a song while I was in there."

"I thought you were done recording," I replied.

Before she got in the passenger seat of Mickie's car, she said, "A true artist is never done."

PTSD is real. I had watched the videos of Paris' outburst at Macy's from multiple angles, and it nearly brought me to tears to see my best friend suffer the symptoms of a disorder she denies having. Her relationship with Brandon was heavy. They were deep in love; they were rich and talented; they were young and spontaneous; and they were living like rock stars. They partied hard, drank too much, and indulged in drugs. And since they were two gorgeous free spirits who were both wanted by males and females all over the world, they also indulged in threesomes. The passion in their relationship was palpable, and when it stemmed from their happiness, it was endearing and to be envied. When influenced by negativity and infidelity, it was catastrophic. They were a beautiful disaster.

Paris had gone through years of emotional trauma with him, but a lot of people chalked it up to them being young and in love, going through the usual relationship drama. Some people closest to her shrugged off the seriousness of their issues because Paris is such a strong woman and they felt like she had things under control. They realized she didn't when the emotional trauma turned physical.

We've been at the club or in the car post-breakup, and YB's music has come on. In the car, we may change the station or sing one of our favorite parts before drowning it out with our conversation. In the club, I've seen her take a shot when his songs come on or quickly down a mixed drink. That, or she'll suddenly take a bathroom break. It's not noticeable to many, but she's my best friend. I know what she's been through. I was the one who applied pressure to her wounds when I found her on her bathroom floor five years ago.

So, when I sat on the bed in my hotel room at the Ritz-Carlton and watched the #turnthatshitoff videos, it was hard for me not to ruin the surprise. I wanted to drive out to Paris and Ricky's house and beg her to go see a therapist. I saw the look in her eyes and the beads of sweat on her forehead. I peeped the subtle tremble of her hand when she spoke into the mic. She's still very much affected by their former relationship. In lieu of going to her house, I texted to see if she was really okay.

Supporting Paris is a no-brainer. She has always looked out for me, and I'll go as far as to say none of the other girls in F.I.R.E. would have paid me any attention had it not been for her. Actually, no one at our school talked to "that fat girl in the LD hallway" until Paris started sitting with me during lunch halfway through our eighth grade year. No one knew I could even sing until Paris overheard me singing D'Angelo's "Brown Sugar" in the lunch line and asked me to join her in the school talent show.

I was so happy to have friends outside of my class-room that I didn't think of how terrifying it would be to get onstage and sing in front of the whole school—not until an hour before show time. That's when Paris stood in front of me and gave me a pep talk I still remember after all these years. She pulled me into a corner backstage, looked into my eyes, and said, "I got you. I'll be right there with you. You can't back out now. This is your moment to show everybody why you're special. It's your voice that makes you special, not that stupid classroom. Just do the same thing you've been doin' in practice."

I took her advice that evening, and my life was for-ever changed. I began singing and performing with her and KiKi at local talent shows and parties. With the addition of Shai the next year, we sparked F.I.R.E. and had an eleven-year run in the industry. F.I.R.E. was more than a group to me. I regard each of the ladies as my sisters, and like biological sisters, we have our unique relationships.

Shai and I have the most similar personalities. We don't say much until prompted to do so, and like her name is pronounced, we're both a little shy. Okay, I'm *very* shy, and the world knows it. It's kind of my "thing." It's what the fans seem to like about me. Now Shai on the other hand, she's shy until she transforms to Tamale, the secret stage name we gave her.

I've probably communicated with Shai the most since she left the group. Why? Because I love her. Yes, it was messed up how she broke up the group, but our split was inevitable. At the time, KiKi was showing up for appearances drunk; Paris was showing up late for everything; and I was more than ready to get from under Zeke's thumb. If anything, Shai had the courage to do what we'd all been thinking about for at least a year.

I saw a different side of Shai because I lived with her for two years. When Zeke found out about my home life with Summer, he talked to Shai's mother, and she welcomed me into their more stable household. During that time, Shai and I did homework together, stayed up late trippin' about the celebrities we were meeting, and fantasized about how F.I.R.E. was going to take over the R&B genre. She taught me how to do my makeup. I would braid her hair. We were tight.

Like most teenage girls, we talked a lot about the boys we were interested in. Shai was raised in the church and determined to hold on to her virginity until marriage. That didn't keep her from being boy crazy, though. It would have been hard for her not to be. She's always been beautiful, and the guys were attracted to her "good girl" ways. Besides Mike from Boyz II Men, I was only interested in one guy at that time. I gave him a different name to protect our relationship: Dino. With his help, I even came up with his fake bio. He was a freshman at Morehouse, was originally from New Jersey, and we met at the mall. I remember the night I told Shai that I'd lost my virginity to him. She wanted all the details, and I provided all except one: I was talking about her uncle. Even now, she has no idea that Dino and Zeke are one and the same.

When I saw Shai in the hotel's fitness center, I knew she had to be a part of Paris' party. I don't believe in coincidences. The universe placed us there because we needed to reconnect. I knew it wouldn't be easy to convince her, Ricky, and KiKi that it was a good idea, but I went for it anyway.

Ricky laughed when I told him. "Oh, wait. You're serious," he said after realizing I wasn't laughing with him. "My bad. I thought you were bullshittin'."

"Does Paris mention Shai to you anymore?" I asked. "I know we don't talk about her, but that could be because I never bring her up."

"Not really. I only hear her mumble about Shai when y'all have to post that fake shit, congratulating her for wipin' her ass," he replied.

"So what do you think? I don't want to have Shai come if Paris is just gonna cuss her out. She might be on a roll after the thing with Brandon."

"Nah. You know your girl be on that tough shit, but she's really soft. If Shai comes out with y'all, that alone will show she's tryna squash their beef. P'll probably respect her for humbling herself. If it goes right, that would be epic. I'm cool with it. Let me know if she says yes, and I'll get her on the list."

Before I called KiKi, I texted Shai to formally invite her. As soon as she asked for the address, I squealed with excitement. F.I.R.E. was going to shock the world with an impromptu reunion. It would be the first time we were all seen together since Paris' wedding.

"Five hundred dollars says she's not coming," KiKi said when I broke the news.

"You might as well transfer it to me now, because she's coming," I replied. "And please be nice."

"I'm not pressed about that girl. I'll be nice, but I'm not gonna pretend like she's there to genuinely celebrate Paris. This is a publicity stunt."

"That's not really fair. I asked her to come."

"And how many times have you asked her to attend other things? Did she ever come to one of your shows? Has she attended your philanthropic events? Nope. You know why? 'Cause you're not her competition. Paris always has been. And since Paris is out here getting some shine again, here comes Shai with the shade. She wants to remind people that she's still the superstar. Next year, she'll have a fragrance. Watch."

I was quiet because the truth stung. No, Shai had never come to my events or shows. She hadn't even shared any of my posts on social media to help promote. I always chalked it up to her being busy, but maybe KiKi was right.

"I'm sorry," KiKi said. "I'm not trying to be negative. This isn't about my dislike for Shai. It's about my protectiveness of you. In my opinion, you give her too much credit. But, I'll say this. It's a great idea. If she shows, I promise to behave. Hopefully, Paris will, too."

I thanked her, then reminded her what time to show up.

"Hold up. You didn't invite Zeke, did you?" she asked.

"No!" I blurted. "I don't know if he's even here. But, if he is and she tries to bring him, he'll be turned away at the door. Ricky's people aren't playing when it comes to that guest list."

"Okay. Just making sure," KiKi said. "I will *not* behave if his slimy ass shows up."

She and Paris knew about my relationship with Zeke. I didn't volunteer the information, but when Paris followed me to the clinic when I got my first abortion, she had already figured it out. Apparently, she and KiKi had speculated I was messing around with Zeke, but they weren't sure. I still talked about Dino during that time, but they could see a bit of favoritism in Zeke's dealings with me. When they would bring it up, I played it off, saying he was like my uncle since I was living with Shai. On the night when I made the decision to terminate my first pregnancy, KiKi and Paris saw me crying as Zeke put cash in my hand. It was after one of our studio sessions when we were recording the *Back for More* album. Zeke and I thought everyone was gone, but apparently, Paris had forgotten her jacket, and they witnessed the transaction. At that point, I didn't know Paris had seen the pregnancy test in my trashcan while she was at my apartment a week prior. I only found out when she called out to me in the abortion center's parking lot and asked why I didn't tell her.

While Paris and KiKi understood the logic that it was not ideal for me to have a child at age seventeen when our careers were just taking off and *with* our manager who was eight years older than me, they lost all respect for him because he was going to let me go through the abortion alone. When I had the second one, KiKi got in my face and his, accusing us of being reckless and inconsiderate concerning each other, the group, and human life. Needless to say, I made sure nobody knew about my third one.

Zeke and I were together off and on for seven years, but I was always his secret. First, we had to creep because of our age difference. He promised when I turned eighteen, we could be seen together. When I turned eighteen, he said it wasn't a good look for the group's image. There was always an excuse, and there were always other women. He claimed they were in place because people would start asking questions if he was never seen with a woman. Back then, I was naïve enough to believe him. It wasn't until I hit rock bottom and was loved back to life that I realized my relationship with Zeke was cancerous. He played on my youth, snatched my innocence, and helped me destroy my womb. After my third abortion, I learned

I would not be able to have a child. Meanwhile, he's moved on and had five.

Thank the Most High for independent adoption. With the help of Paris and her lawyer, I was blessed with a beautiful baby girl. I was able to witness her arrival into this world. I stood right there in the delivery room and listened to her cry for the first time. I sat next to her incubator in the NICU and sang to her. I even had the pleasure of naming her. And since the adoption was done independently, privacy was no issue.

Journey came into my life when I needed to be rejuvenated. While I helped save her life, she helped validate mine. Though she didn't come from my womb, our love is effortless and reciprocal. She is my baby, and I'm her mom. Since she was almost taken from this world, I'm determined to give her the world.

Paris and I sat on the couch while my mother struggled with her lyrics in the booth. I had done as she asked and booked her two days of studio time. She spent the first day arguing with the engineer about his capabilities. I told her that she needed to be productive on day two because that was all the money I was going to spend. As an artist, I understand her need to keep her creative juices flowing, but I don't have thousands of dollars to waste.

"This beat is hot," Paris said, bobbing her head.

"If you only knew what it took to get this far," I

replied, shaking mine. "I'm glad you decided to come."

"Of course. You know Summer is my girl. I wanted to pop in and see what was stewing in her this time. I see she's feeling jazzy." Paris snapped her fingers and moved her upper body to the rhythm.

Summer noticed Paris grooving and pumped her fist in the air.

"Ayyye! Get it, Summer!" Paris cheered, then turned her attention back to me for a moment. "So you think she's gonna stay clean this time?"

I shrugged and pressed my hands together to symbolize prayer. "She said she's too old to be out there getting high. We'll see. So far, so good."

Paris watched her in awe. "She will. Look at her. She looks happy."

I gave her another few seconds to vibe to the music before redirecting her to the main reason we were meeting. "So…" I purposely let the word hang in the atmosphere.

She rolled her eyes. "So everybody is down for real?"

We had all been overwhelmed by the response to the birthday footage. We basically broke the internet the night of Paris' party. Days later, our managers were getting phone calls, our DMs were blowing up, and it was no longer easy to run to Publix to get groceries without being noticed. F.I.R.E. was hot again, and we weren't even back together—at least not yet.

Christian Watts, super producer and the man responsible for introducing F.I.R.E. to the world, called KiKi after he saw our birthday serenade online. He told her that we really need to let go of the past and get back to making money together. He also said he'd like to be a part of the project if we made another album.

I nodded. "To at least have a real conversation? Yes. We're just waiting on you."

"So Shai Renee Burton-Hartsgrove is seriously considering this? My time is too valuable to play games with her. Don't get me wrong. Y'all sounded amazing and we had a moment on that stage, but what's making her consider reuniting *this* time?"

"I don't know. Growth? I can't speak for her. That's why we all need to sit down and talk. We all claim to be grown women. We should be able to have a productive conversation and move on."

"Well, I'm telling you now I'm not working with Zeke's punk ass. If that's a deal-breaker, y'all need to ca-all Simo-one. Call her!" she sang to the tune of Erykah Badu's song, "Tyrone."

"We know how that worked out last time," I replied.

Simone was the chick Zeke found to replace Paris when we first tried to reunite. Our fans did not appreciate her presence, and she was gone before we even recorded with her.

Paris shrugged. "Or y'all could perform as a trio if I'm the odd woman out. It was the three of y'all onstage at my party anyway."

"You know we're not doing that. F.I.R.E. isn't F.I.R.E. without all four *original* members."

"So have y'all thought about who should manage us then?"

92

"Well, not really."

"'Cause I don't think any of our current managers should manage the group. It'll be too easy for broads to cry favoritism. We should probably hit up Crystal Moss," Paris suggested.

"Dante's wife?" I confirmed.

Paris nodded. "You know she's been managing him for like five or six years now. That dude is still booked after all these years in the business *and* a herpes scandal. She manages Red Bottoms, 317, and a few other people, too. Ricky had considered her at one time."

"Oh, wow."

"And I'ma need—"

I held up my hand. "So I guess this means you're willing to come to the table for a discussion?"

I chuckled and so did Paris.

She sighed. "When is it?"

# EPILOGUE

2 MONTHS LATER...

**O**ne by one, Paris, Reign, KiKi, and Shai arrived in their respective cars. At almost ten o'clock in the morning, the sun was at full-shine, justifying the sunglasses mounted on their faces. However, the accessories best served to hide their truths rather than block UV rays. The women agreed to meet at the Four Seasons in Atlanta, neutral ground for negotiating. If all went well, F.I.R.E. would reunite to record one last studio album and embark on a nationwide tour.

As usual, KiKi was the first to arrive, wearing Adidas leggings and an oversized shirt. It was the easiest outfit to slip on after her night of acrobatics with Christian. She wore her baseball cap as low as her shades would allow and hoped her walk didn't reflect the pain she still felt between her legs. In one hand, she carried her leather portfolio and cell phone. Once inside, she was going to use her other hand to carry the alcoholic beverage she planned to order. It was five o'clock somewhere, and considering the conversations that were bound to take place, she would most likely ask for a double.

Reign held her phone against her ear as she entered the hotel. Journey had forgotten her violin at home and was begging Reign to bring it to the school. Her second grade orchestra concert was that evening, and she needed it for rehearsal. Reign felt guilty. If they hadn't been out until two a.m. looking for Summer, perhaps both of them would have been more alert when they started their day at six. Unfortunately, there was nothing she could do. Mackenzie was on-set in New Orleans, and she was the only person other than Paris who had a spare key to the house. Reign hung up and took a sip of her latte before asking an employee for guidance to the meeting room. Between her daughter and mother, the morning had already been stressful. She could only imagine those interactions were merely preludes to what would take place in minutes.

Paris exited her car debuting her new blonde tresses beneath a slouchy beanie. In an effort to go unnoticed, she kept her head down, pretending to text on her phone. She was steps away from the door when a male voice called her name from an SUV toward the back of the valet line. His Italian accent rang familiar in her ears. When she turned her head, Andrea's sexy smile greeted her. She walked toward the vehicle, and he got out of the passenger seat to meet her halfway.

"Wow," she said as they hugged and exchanged pecks on each other's cheeks. "Mr. Bianchi. It's been a while."

"It has," he said, adjusting a lock of her hair. "Bellissimo. Still."

"Grazie," she said behind a childlike smile.

When she asked, he explained that he was in town to discuss a last-minute coaching opportunity with Atlanta United. She was happy to hear he was still involved with soccer after retiring from his sixteen-year career as defensive midfielder a few years prior. They'd met at the FIFA World Cup in 1998 when he was in his prime.

Before she could fill him in on her happenings, Shai called her name.

"And is that Dre? OMG!" Shai scurried over to them in her six-inch red bottoms and kissed Andrea on his cheeks, then gave Paris a quick side hug. "What are—?"

"It was good to see you," Paris said to Andrea. "We have a meeting to get to."

"How long is your meeting? I can see you after," Andrea said.

"I'm not really sure. And honestly, I might be all talked out by the time we're done."

"I'm staying here for the week. Maybe we can have dinner," he replied.

Paris grabbed his hand and held it briefly. "We both know that's not a good idea. It was good to see you," she said again.

She slowly let his hand go as she walked away. Shai accompanied her.

"Ooh wee! Brava, girl. Don't bite the apple," Shai said as they navigated to the meeting room.

"Shit, I wanted to climb every inch of that six-foot-two tree and bite every one of his apples," Paris admitted.

"Not be fruitful and multiply!"

"Listen."

They laughed and instinctively touched fingertips in agreeance. Shai's stomach settled a bit. Though things had gone well at Paris' birthday celebration, she hadn't been in contact with Paris or KiKi. All communication took place between Zeke and their managers. Shai had only spoken directly to Reign, who wanted to make sure she was truly open to sitting down to hash out their differences.

"Well, this is familiar," Reign said as Paris and Shai entered the room. "Showing up late, giggling like you haven't kept everybody waiting. This may be a good sign."

Paris flipped up her middle finger in response.

"Good morning, everybody," Shai said.

"We didn't know you were bringing Marilyn Monroe along," KiKi quipped.

Paris flung her hair over her shoulder, almost hitting

KiKi in the face. "Now you know." She rounded the table and sat next to Reign.

Shai settled in the chair next to KiKi and placed her trembling hands in her lap. The vibe was good—not great, but good—and she was certain she had made a terrible mistake that was sure to ruin it. In a last-minute effort to keep the spirit of sisterhood intact, she pulled out her phone and sent a quick text message.

Everyone joked about KiKi drinking a margarita with her bagel, recalling the times she'd snuck alcohol on their tour bus when they were only sixteen and seventeen. That led to more stories—about the boys in Pittsburgh who snuck into their dressing room, the time when four of Shai's box braids fell out onstage, and when Reign walked in on Paris and Andrea having sex in the kitchen. They were all in tears, laughing at their tomfoolery.

"Speaking of Dre…" Paris' voice trailed off.

KiKi perked up. "What? Did he DM you?"

Paris opened her mouth to answer, but was distracted by an unexpected attendee. "I thought we said no managers at this first meeting."

KiKi and Shai turned toward the door. Reign looked up from her phone and her heart dropped. Zeke strolled into the room and sat on the other side of Shai. He offered a general hello to everyone, but his eyes lingered when he looked at Reign. She cut her eyes back to her phone. She hadn't seen Zeke in five years—not in person—and life was moving along just fine. Never did she anticipate it would feel like someone slammed on the brakes when she saw him face to face again.

Her reaction took her by surprise. First of all, he looked amazing. At age forty-four, he looked distinguished with his salt and pepper goatee and chinstrap. And fine. He was still fine. The moisture in her panties was proof of that. She hadn't been affected in that way by a man since the early 2000's…since him. Ironically, he was also the one who had made her look the other way. He was often manipulative and disrespectful during their secret relationship. Sometimes, he was downright mean. But, she'd been told there's something about your first love that makes you cherish the warm and fuzzy feelings even though they may not have lasted. As she sat at the table, she could attest to the accuracy of that statement.

"We did say no managers," KiKi confirmed.

"Ladies, let's not do that. Without me, this doesn't go down," Zeke replied.

KiKi's nostrils flared as she shot daggers at him with her eyes.

"You don't own the rights to a damn thing, so you don't determine whether this goes down," Paris clarified. "You are entitled to your percentage of F.I.R.E.'s earnings, and that's it."

"You can't have a reunion without performing your old music," Zeke said with a shrug. "Christian owns the rights to the majority of your songs, and I'm sure if he knows I'm not on-board with this reunion, you ladies won't have anything to sing for your fans.

And even if he does support, you'll be singing them without the hottest R&B/Pop singer in the game." He glanced at Shai and looked back at Paris.

KiKi smiled slightly. Though Christian and Zeke were close friends back when F.I.R.E. started, she knew Christian didn't have the staunch loyalty to him that Zeke was implying. He was, however, loyal to making money and having great sex. They had done both together over the years, so she wasn't concerned.

She was concerned about Shai's involvement, though. The truth was there could be no reunion without her. And with Shai's puppet master sitting next to her and threatening to take her out of the equation, KiKi wondered if the whole thing was a setup to bully them into letting Zeke manage the group again.

Shai was upset with herself. She didn't officially invite Zeke to come, but she knew when she told him that she was meeting with the ladies, he would want to as well. A part of her didn't want him there because the dynamic between him and the other ladies was volatile at best, but the other part of her relied on him as her security blanket. She trusted he had her best interest in mind, and if he was there, she wouldn't make such a major decision with her heart rather than her head. It wasn't until she was in the same room with everyone again that she realized there was no need for backup.

"You knew he was coming?" Paris asked Shai.

"He was aware I was coming," Shai replied.

Reign sighed and shook her head. "That's not what she asked you."

"Same ol' shit," Paris said. She turned to Reign. "I kept my end of the bargain. I came to the table. But, I warned you that I wasn't fuckin' with him." She stood up and reached for her purse.

Reign grabbed her wrist and held it.

"Go ahead and let Flo Jo leave. That's what she's great at—running." Zeke laughed.

Paris wanted to tell him what he was good at, but Reign's sweaty hand gripping her wrist made her think before she spoke. She looked at Shai instead. "You just couldn't follow the one rule we had, huh?"

"This isn't what—"

"Don't even insult us with the lie you're about to tell," KiKi said.

"You're shady as hell. What was your endgame? Are we gonna walk outside and find a thousand paparazzi waiting for you to announce that the reunion didn't work out but your new album will drop in twenty minutes?" Paris asked.

"Phony ass. You're right, P. She probably used us again. That's what *she's* good at," KiKi directed at Zeke.

"Ladies," Reign attempted.

Shai was appalled. "Use y'all? Do you see me out here struggling as a solo artist?"

"You will always be Shai from F.I.R.E., girl. Be humble," Paris said.

"And if you're going to call me phony, I can say the same about y'all," Shai continued. "You've got all this to say now that we've come together in private, but I'll be damned if y'all aren't on social media shouting me out and congratulating me on everything I do."

"Bitch, you think we do that shit because we *want* to? Have you forgotten that in 2008, your uncle had us sign this bullshit contract that requires us to publicly support you?" KiKi pulled the contract from her portfolio. "Miss me with that 'phony' shit. We were being obedient," KiKi added.

"Oh wow. She brought the shut-the-fuck-up papers with her," Paris said under her breath. She lowered herself back into her seat, sure not to miss the remainder of the meeting.

Reign hung her head as KiKi pushed the papers in Shai's direction. Zeke cleared his throat and inter-twined his fingers. The ladies watched as Shai read the clause KiKi was referring to.

Left and right, her eyes scanned the paragraph—quickly at first, then again slowly. With egg on her face, she looked at everyone in the room one by one. All these years, she thought her former group members were following her career and cheering her success because they had moved on from their anger and were proud of her, only to have six sentences reveal they were obligated to do so—angry or not.

"That was put in place to protect you, babygirl," Zeke started. "A gag clause alone isn't enough. Silence speaks volumes. The media reads through that. Since they were acknowledging you, it made it seem like—"

"A lie," Shai offered. "It was all a lie."

"This is a business, Shai. I've stressed that to you from the time you all got your deal. Personal matters and business matters must remain separate."

"You made sure of that. Seems like your advice separated me from my friends."

Paris had to chime in. "He helped, but you need to own your part. You acted like you were responsible for F.I.R.E.'s success and we were your background singers. You separated yourself. He made sure it stayed that way."

"I was in my twenties, Paris. You of all people can attest to the mistakes we made in our twenties."

Paris smirked. "Here we go with this shit."

"You never apologized in your thirties, Shai," Reign spoke up. "You never made amends."

"So if I say I'm sorry, we can all move on? Is it that simple?" Shai asked.

"Not if you're saying it to shut us up," Reign answered.

Zeke glanced down at his Rolex. "Is this a therapy session or a meeting about a reunion?"

Reign's phone vibrated on the table. She looked at the screen to see it was Leanne calling. "Excuse me, everybody. I have to take this." She got up from the table and stepped outside the meeting room. "Hey, Aunt LeeLee," she answered as she closed the door behind her.

"It's a meeting you weren't invited to," Paris said to Zeke.

"You should be happy anyone would even consider working with you again," Zeke stated smugly.

"And you should be happy you were never locked

up for statutory rape. But karma's a bitch. How old are your daughters?" she asked.

"Whoa! What is that about? And that's an all-time low for you to bring children into adult matters, Paris," Shai said.

Zeke's jaw was clenched tightly as he glared at Paris.

"You remember Dino?" KiKi asked Shai.

Shai's brow furrowed, displaying her confusion. "Yeah. Reign's ex. Why?"

Zeke tried to butt in. "Shai—"

"Well, there was no Dino. She was really messing with—"

"Noooo!" Reign's cry could be heard clearly through the door.

Everyone ran into the hallway to see what was wrong. Zeke was the first out the door. They arrived just in time to see Reign slide down the wall and crumple to the floor. She curled into the fetal position and sobbed.

Paris pushed past Zeke and dropped to her knees next to Reign. "What happened?"

Reign only cried harder when she tried to speak, making every word unintelligible. Paris wrapped her arms around her and rocked her slightly, hoping to calm her down.

Zeke noticed Reign's phone was in the opposite corner, and the call was still active. As he got closer to it, he could hear Leanne calling out to Reign. No sooner than he picked up the phone, KiKi snatched it out of his hand.

"Hello?" she said into the phone. "No, this is KiKi."

Paris braced herself for the news as Reign grabbed a fistful of her shirt. There was only one thing that could upset Reign to that extent. She closed her eyes, waiting for the last piece of information. She knew the "what." Her question was "Who?"

Tears welled up in KiKi's eyes as she listened to Leanne on the other end of the line.

"Okay. Yes, ma'am. We'll get her there. Thank you."

She ended the call and looked at Paris. "Summer," she said.

Tears ran down Paris' cheeks as she shook her head.

KiKi nodded and tears fell from her eyes, as well. "She's dead."

Reign followed her mother's wishes to a T. Summer's funeral was held outside at the cemetery. In lieu of flowers, guests donated to her favorite charitable organization, Tostan, using iPads set up next to the sign-in book; and to honor her last request, everyone wore denim bottoms, white tops, and sandals—the specified outfit if she passed away during spring or summer months.

The turnout was overwhelming. Summer had touched many lives, and people traveled from across the country and some from across the world to come pay their respects. Fellow musicians, record company execs, ex-boyfriends, and former neighbors and nurses filled the chairs along with other friends and family.

A representative from Tostan even attended and told Reign how she'd only spoken to her mother over the phone, but appreciated all the money she had donated to their cause over the years.

The most comforting presence was that of her sisters. Shai, Paris, and KiKi never left her side during the waking hours from the time she received the news of Summer's death until the funeral. They sorted through Summer's belongings, helped write her obituary, shooed away the press, and lent their shoulders for Reign to dampen. Even with all of their assistance, Reign was exhausted. She couldn't wait for the repast to end so she could go home and get some rest.

"Hey, babes. You look worn out. What can we do to help?" Paris asked as she walked toward her. Shai and KiKi followed.

"Can you bring her back?" Reign asked, attempting to crack a smile.

Paris stood toe-to-toe with her friend and leaned in so their foreheads touched. "You know how people say your loved ones will live on inside of you when they pass? I really do believe that. She's not gone. She's forever in your heart. Mine, too."

She stepped aside and held Reign's hand for reassurance.

"I really appreciate all of you being here for me," Reign said to KiKi and Shai, choking up a bit.

"Where else would we be?" Shai asked.

"Summer was our mama, too," KiKi said. "And she kept us from being broke."

They laughed. Reign did, too, but the memories of her mother with the group caused the levees of her eyes to break. Summer was looking forward to them reuniting. It was all she talked about after she'd gotten out of rehab the last time. Certain that the ladies would squash old beef and focus on making music together again, Summer had jotted down ideas for the tour name, song titles, and marketing ideas. Yet, the day Reign learned Summer was dead was the same day she realized F.I.R.E. was dead, too.

"Despite our differences, we were friends before we were F.I.R.E.," Shai said. "I know I've been out of the loop, but that's over. I'm sure I speak for everyone when I say we'll be whatever you need us to be and help you get through this however we can. That's what friends do."

Piggybacking off of Shai's last sentence, Paris started singing the chorus of "That's What Friends Are For" to Reign, hugging her from behind and swaying to the beat. Shai and KiKi instinctively joined her, harmonizing where appropriate. In thirty seconds, they had captured the attention of everyone who remained in the reception hall. They giggled and cried amid the unexpected applause, slightly embarrassed that others witnessed what was supposed to be a private moment.

Paris really did mean the words she sang. Reign was one of her best friends—more like her sister—and Summer was her second mother. She was the cool mom in comparison to her biological mother who didn't understand the "music thing" and wished she would pursue a career in chemistry instead. Summer understood her wild side, only she referred to it as her freedom cry. They had smoked weed and written songs together. Summer even bailed Paris out of jail when she was arrested for trespassing at YB's house. Instead of chastising her, Summer directed Paris to Egypt for holistic restoration. She could see Paris was spiraling out of control and recommended that the beautiful district of Zamalek be her home for a year. During her time away, Paris kept in touch with a few people, but no one knew her whereabouts except Summer.

Paris remembered one of their talks from that time. Summer told her that she wouldn't live to see age sixty. She was a firm believer that everyone had a specific expiration date on Earth, and she knew her purpose would be served before she reached sixty years. She also told Paris that she would die unpredictably, and she was right. Everyone's first thought was that she had died from a drug overdose, but she'd actually died from a freak accident in Leanne's guest bathroom.

Shai was grateful for her nanny who flew into Atlanta with her little ones so Shai could be there for Reign. She hated that the air hadn't been cleared with everyone since the meeting, but there was no way she was leaving Reign's side during such a troubling time. She knew how complicated Reign's relationship was with her mother and imagined Summer's death affected Reign on multiple levels. Singing the snippet of the song took her back to her mother's house in Union City when Reign lived with them. Too many nights, Shai would console Reign as she cried herself to sleep, wondering where Summer was and if she was in danger. As she stood holding Reign's hand in the reception hall, a wave of love fell over her. She missed this. She missed sisterhood.

KiKi's wheels were turning. Paris' impromptu serenade was genius. If F.I.R.E. could've reunited, that song would have been perfect for their new CD. It made sense. The song truly did embody their friendship, even if not in the present. They sounded phenomenal singing it, even with the minimal effort they put into it. And it could appeal to a wide audience. It was a classic that could easily be resurrected and slightly remixed with the help of Christian. And if they could get Stevie Wonder to play the harmonica...

Her daydream was interrupted when some of the guests approached to tell them how great they sounded. They thanked the strangers for the compliments and continued with their conversations—Reign with Shai, and Paris with KiKi. Shortly thereafter, Leanne, Mackenzie, and Journey broke up their huddle.

"I came over here to audition," Mackenzie joked as she made her way over to Reign. "I can be the Elton John of the group."

Laughter ensued.

Journey walked to Paris' side and wrapped her arms around Paris' waist. Paris kissed her goddaughter's forehead and stroked her hair.

"Can I stay with you tonight?" Journey asked. "I already asked Uncle Ricky, and he said it's okay with him."

Paris looked over at Reign, who had already heard her daughter's question.

"I don't care," Reign replied.

"Slumber party!" Journey and Paris started chanting and did the Nae Nae while the others looked on with amusement.

"Sometimes I think they're both seven," Reign said, shaking her head.

"Before this turns into a full-fledged dance party, let me step in real quick and say this. You ladies sounded incredible," Leanne expressed. "And I want to put this out there 'cause it's on my heart. I know you were just having fun, but you really have a gift—a *collective* gift. Summer had a saying: 'Life is too short to wait for the perfect time...'"

"'...and too long to say you don't have time,'" Shai, KiKi, and Paris said in unison, finishing the statement with Leanne.

"Y'all aren't done yet. We all witnessed it here. Don't let your gift go to waste," Leanne advised.

"We aren't," Shai blurted. "I'm thinking that song should be the first single off our reunion album." She looked at her other group members. "What do y'all think?"

Reign's eyes widened and her brows rose. "For real?" she asked.

Shai winked. "For real."

"Without...?" KiKi asked.

"Without Zeke," Shai confirmed.

KiKi pulled her phone from her purse. "Well, I think I'm telling Christian to get ready 'cause F.I.R.E.

has reignited!" She started a celebratory dance but stopped abruptly. "P, you still down? What you think?"

"I think Reign better start practicing our old choreography now, with her non-dancing ass," Paris said nonchalantly as she dodged Reign's hit.

"Don't talk about my baby," Mackenzie said while laughing.

"Mom, you do need a little help in the dancing department," Journey added.

"Et tu?" Reign said, playfully shaking her daughter.

Paris calmed her laughter and nudged Reign. "No, really, I'm down. Let's do it in memory of Summer."

That's it?
Of course not!
Read about the events that led
· Paris, Shai, Kiki, and Reign
**Through The F.I.R.E. (a novel)**,
Coming 2018.
Until then, here's a sneak peek.

·

# A SEAT AT THE TABLE

## 1996

**T**HE cafeteria was abuzz with gossip. The fight everyone had been waiting for all week had taken place right before B Lunch, and it was everything the students hoped for. Slim had just gotten out of juvenile hall, and he'd vowed to beat the truth out of Floyd for making false accounts that landed him there. If the truth came out by way of blood, Slim had more than accomplished his goal. Floyd was in route to the hospital, and Slim was most likely headed to juvie again.

LeToya and Natina sat at their usual table and recapped the brawl.

"You think they can put his tooth back in?" LeToya asked, referring to Floyd.

"*Teeth*, you mean," Natina corrected. "I saw three on the floor,"

"Dang!"

"But I don't know. They had Mr. Lang run down here and get some milk. I heard Nurse Alford say she needed it for Floyd's teeth."

"Where's Paris?" LeToya asked, craning her neck.

"She went to the payphone to call Slim's mama after he threw the first punch. I haven't seen her since," Natina replied.

In the lunch line, Reign swiveled her head to the beat of the music in her headphones. As the lunch ladies placed food on her tray, she thanked each of them and followed behind the rest of her classmates. While walking toward her usual table, she noticed Natina and waved shyly. Natina smiled and waved back, and then continued her conversation with LeToya.

Reign couldn't believe one of the coolest girls in eighth grade acknowledged her twice in one day. And she was nice both times. Just minutes before, Natina stopped her from walking into the middle of Slim and Floyd's fight zone. They even had a quick conversation about the reason for the fight before parting ways.

Reign longed to make new friends. Sure, she liked the kids in her class, but it was often hard to communicate with them due to their speech delays or behavioral issues. For some reason, some of the students who were in other classrooms barely acknowledged her; and if they did, it was because they were in P.E. and had to participate in an activity together.

Her mother blamed it on her being too quiet and encouraged her to be more outgoing. Easier said than done...until today.

"Mrs. Gamble, can I sit over there?" Reign asked, pointing to the table where Natina was.

Mrs. Gamble barely took her attention away from the boy who was already seated and eating mashed potatoes with his fingers. "Is there a seat over there, Reign?"

"Yes. A bunch."

"Then go ahead."

Before Mrs. Gamble's sentence was complete, Reign was just feet away from the empty seat next to Natina.

"Hey, y'all. Can I sit here?" she asked with a big smile.

Just as she placed her tray on the table, Natina opened her mouth to speak.

"Somebody's sitting there, Headphones," LeToya answered.

"Oh, okay," Reign replied. She slid her tray across the table, next to LeToya's.

LeToya slid it back toward her before she could walk around. "Here, too." She pulled her crossbody purse over her head and placed it where the tray was. "In fact, all of these seats are taken. Sorry."

Natina apologized, too, but with a bit of sincerity. "Lunchroom seats kinda become assigned seats. You know? But there's plenty of seats over there by your friends."

"Right. Go on back to the LD table," LeToya mumbled.

Reign looked at the four other vacant seats near the girls that were usually empty from one day to the next. She got the picture. She wasn't wanted there. With her head down, she picked up her tray and started to walk away. Upon her quick exit, she bumped the end of the table and stumbled a bit.

LeToya burst into laughter but tried to stifle it. Natina kicked her under the table, but giggled a bit, too. Suddenly Reign had more attention on her than she'd ever wanted. She made it to her usual seat at the opposite end of the table where her classmates ate and picked at the food she no longer had an appetite for.

"What y'all laughin' at?" Paris asked moments later as she set her tray down and took her seat next to Natina.

"She's laughing because she's rude, and I'm laughing at how hard she's laughing," Natina explained.

LeToya gathered herself so she could speak. "Un unh. Tina's over here attracting the LD kids. I had to shoo one away."

"What? Who came over here?" Paris asked, instinctively laughing with her friends.

"Headphones," LeToya answered.

"What did she do?"

"Nothing. She just wanted to sit by me. I think she thought we were friends or something 'cause I stopped her from walking into Slim's fist during the fight. You know she doesn't really pay attention," Natina explained.

"I'm still lost. What's so funny? Where's she at?" Paris questioned.

"Her regular seat," Natina said.

"The funny part is when she walked away and…"

As LeToya recounted Reign almost falling, Paris stared across the cafeteria at the girl her friends had snubbed. Reign sat alone with her headphones on, moving her food around the tray but not eating. Paris looked at the empty seat next to her and the three others next to LeToya.

She snapped out of her trance while LeToya was still talking. "Y'all told her she couldn't sit here?"

"Yeah," LeToya said. "She was about to sit in your seat."

"That's weak. You see all these other seats here." She shook her head and took a bite of her food.

"Excuse me! I didn't know she was your homie," LeToya fired back.

"She ain't gotta be my homie."

"Then you must be trippin' 'cause Slim is about to be locked up again. You got an attitude with us over nothin'."

"This ain't got nothin' to do with Slim. What y'all did was whack. That girl don't bother nobody. All she does is listen to whatever's playing through those headphones, and she minds her business." She swallowed her food and turned to Natina. "On the real, you probably made her day earlier. Then just like that, you jacked it up. She ain't even eatin'."

Reign wasn't even holding a utensil anymore. With her tray pushed aside and one elbow propped on the table, she rested her chin in the palm of her hand and stared at the clock. Her other hand played with the cord attached to her headphones. She didn't have friends, but she had music. She always had music. And as she waited for the bell to ring, she let the sound of Monica's "Don't Take It Personal" drown out the echo of LeToya and Natina's hurtful words.

"Did you ask your mom if you can come over after school?" LeToya asked as she handed her tray to the lunch lady.

Paris shook her head. "I'm meeting up with KiKi. We gotta practice for the Christmas showcase."

"So y'all really gonna do it? You think you can win?" LeToya asked.

"Damn skippy they can win it!" Natina answered.

Paris shrugged and smiled. "I guess we'll see."

"Did y'all pick a name?" Natina asked.

Wearing a smirk across her lips, Paris replied, "Cookies & Cream."

As they high-fived each other, Natina bumped into Reign, who was reaching into the cooler for a carton of milk. "My bad!" Natina said as she turned to see who she'd made contact with. "Oh, hey!" she added once she saw it was Reign.

Reign kept her head down and scurried to her seat.

"Dang! She didn't even say anything to you," LeToya joked. "You got played by the slow girl."

Natina elbowed her as they grabbed their milk and headed to their table.

Paris couldn't take her eyes off of Reign. It had

been that way for more than a week, ever since her friends told her how they'd refused to let Reign sit with them. Until that conversation, she hadn't paid much attention to the quiet girl from the "special" hallway who always wore headphones.

After receiving her full tray from the last server, Paris started in the direction of her friends. Halfway to their table, she stopped. "Hey!" she called, getting LeToya and Natina's attention. "Y'all go 'head. I'll see y'all in computer class."

"Where are you sitting?" Natina asked as Paris walked in the opposite direction.

Her question was answered seconds later when Paris carefully approached Reign. She and LeToya looked on in disbelief.

Paris stood next to the seat directly across from Reign and pointed to it. "You care if I sit here?" she asked.

Reign pulled the earpiece away from her left ear. "What did you say?"

"This seat. Is it cool if I sit here?" Paris asked again.

"I don't care," Reign said. The apprehension in her voice was clear as she peeked around Paris to get a clear view of seat availability in the cafeteria. There were more open seats than Reign cared to count, including Paris' usual one next to Natina.

Paris smiled as she sat down. "I'm Paris."

Reign nodded and removed the headphones.

"You already knew that?" After Reign's second nod, Paris said, "Well, now I feel bad. I only know you as Headphones. What's your real name?"

Reign looked in LeToya and Natina's direction again. Both girls had been staring, but they diverted their eyes as soon as Reign's glance met their gaze. Paris looked over her shoulder to see who or what was preoccupying Reign.

"My friends told me what happened the other day. I don't think it was cool. And since you have all this room over here, I wanted to come sit with you," Paris explained.

"Reign."

"Huh?"

"It's Reign."

Remembering that Reign had some type of special need, Paris tried to redirect her. "No, I don't think it's raining outside today. It's supposed to rain this weekend, though. But I was asking—"

"My *name* is Reign — like a queen or king rules over a country."

Paris laughed. "Oh snap! I feel stupid. Okay! That's fly!"

Reign couldn't help but giggle. "Thank you. My mom named me."

They exchanged stories about their unique names. Paris shared how her mother named her and her sister, India, after places she'd dreamed of visiting. Reign revealed that her father was Egyptian, and she was named Reign because Egypt is the land of kings and queens.

"He's *for real* Egyptian?" Paris asked.

Reign nodded. "That's where my mom met him. He's dead now, though."

"I'm sorry. That's a cool-ass story, though. I think you have me beat," Paris replied.

The girls laughed and continued chatting, oblivious to the numerous sets of eyes watching their interaction. Paris was surprised to learn how well-traveled Reign was and how knowledgeable she was about the places she'd been — within the U.S. and internationally. While she had posters of the Eiffel Tower in her room, Reign had actually stood next to it.

The ringing bell ended their conversation before either of them were ready. Paris told Reign they would pick up where they left off the next day. Though Reign said okay, she wasn't counting on Paris sitting with her again.

As they walked to the tray return area, Mrs. Gamble stopped Paris and pulled her aside. "That was sweet what you did. I'm sure Reign appreciated you sitting with her."

Mrs. Gamble was familiar with Paris. She was the French Club sponsor, and Paris was a member. She knew Paris to be extremely intelligent and outgoing. She was a born leader and was well-liked. Because Paris was an influencer among her peers, Mrs. Gamble was impressed that she had set a positive example of inclusion, whether she realized it or not.

Paris smiled. "It's all good. Reign is pretty cool. Real smart. I told her I'll come sit with her again."

"You should. You may be surprised at how much you have in common." Mrs. Gamble winked before turning to help her students put their trays away.

Off the top of her head, Paris couldn't think of anything they'd have in common other than their distinctive names. Then again, she never thought she would sit across from Reign and have an engaging conversation. So, she didn't want to underestimate the possibilities. Because she loved science, she wondered if that's what Mrs. Gamble was referring to. Maybe Reign was also into molecules and elements. Or could Reign speak French? Intrigued, Paris was determined to learn more about Reign; and it would be easy since they'd have time to talk during lunch from that day forward.

Who is Crystal?

Here's a hint...if you've read

**The Disgruntled Wives Club**

by Portia A. Cosby,

You Already Know Who She Is.

If Not, Meet Crystal, Circa 2008.

What happens when the
lines are blurred between
*I do and I don't?*

# The Disgruntled Wives Club
### A NOVEL

# PORTIA A. COSBY

# excerpt from
# The Disgruntled Wives Club

## *Crystal*

I stood at the side of the stage with Milky and Dana, waiting for the smoke to clear. Dante had completed his third wardrobe change and now wore charcoal-gray silk pajama pants, baby oil, and a look in his eyes that would send every female into panty-dropping mode.

The women in the crowd went wild as my husband gyrated onstage and crooned to the crying fan in the front row. The excitement I felt reminded me of the first three years of our marriage when I proudly hung on his arm as the woman who snagged the hottest R&B sensation of the era. Now that we've reached year eight of matrimony, I see him for what he really is: an actor. If those women only knew he has acne that flares up once a month like a woman on her period, won't shave his hairy balls, and can't live up to his lyrics about lovemaking, they wouldn't be standing with wet panties wishing he was theirs.

When he first wrote "Mr. All Night Long" and let me hear it one night before we went to bed, I loved it. It's one of those songs you can put on your "get some" CD twice. The problem is, I can only get some from him once, and nowadays, I have to cheat and apply my clit stimulating cream before we make love if I want to guarantee an orgasm.

Let him tell it, his lackluster bedroom performances are a side effect of his larger-than-life stage performances. He's either too tired to even try and I end up on top doing all the work, or he flops on top of me repeatedly and pauses for extended breaks, or he gives his last ten-minute burst of energy that ends with him shriveling up inside of me when I'm just warming up.

Let me tell it, he's been doing more than he's previously admitted to with his little groupies. His mannerisms are more informal; he's not as explosive when he cums; and his stamina has decreased far more than he can blame on fatigue. If it's that serious, drink a Red Bull and let's get it poppin'.

I watched Dante pull the little hot girl on stage and sit her in the chair. 'Privileged' was written all over her face as she winked at her girlfriends in the crowd and puckered her lips at my husband. Her miniskirt barely met her mid-thigh, and when she crossed her right leg over her left, it crept up two more inches. Dante complimented her on her choice of wardrobe, then asked the men in the audience if they agreed.

*Game on.* Just as he did to the blonde in Phoenix, the plus-size beauty in New Orleans, and the ebony woman in Houston, he stood in front of the P.Y.T. and sang to her. Starting with a stroke of her hair, he made that stranger feel special. His hand never left her body as he lowered himself to his knees.

I miss the exciting Dante. Before we ever met, I would see him around town—sometimes at Lafayette Square Mall, other times at the skating rink on the Westside, but mostly at the StarQuest competitions where he'd perform with three of his high school friends. From Jodeci to Boyz II Men to Shai, their renditions of the time's hottest music had us teenage girls open.

Dante always stood out. He was the best looking, the best vocalist, and the best dancer. So, imagine how many females became instant Crystal haters when Dante and I crossed paths again during my freshman year of college. Just add jealousy and stir.

It was homecoming, and he came to IU to perform. His visit was a big deal because he's an Indiana native who had just signed his first record contract. I was working at the sports complex at the time, and Saturday morning, I had to open the place. When I arrived at 5:40 a.m., ten minutes late as usual, Dante and his manager, Tre, were waiting by the main doors.

"Do you work here, sweetie?" Tre asked.

I didn't answer because there's no way he could've missed me placing my key in the door and opening it.

"You look familiar," Dante said, squinting as if it would somehow help his memory. "Are you from Nap?"

Being too tired to care that he recognized me, I nodded and held the door open. "Are y'all coming in?"

As they followed me to the main office, I asked if they were coming to work out.

Tre cleared his throat and activated his let's-make-a-deal voice. "That's what we're hoping to do. See, I don't know if you know who this young man is, but he's one of the hottest new—"

"His name is Dante, and he's performing tonight at Assembly Hall." I turned to Dante. "Are you trying to work out for free? Is that what he's trying to get at?"

After a nervous laugh, he nodded. "Can you get me in? I'm not feeling the fitness center at the hotel, and I don't like missing my workouts."

I glanced to see if my boss was looking, then activated the turnstile so they could go through.

"I appreciate it," Dante said.

I didn't appreciate the smile he had given me until an hour later when I woke up completely. Once he was done working out, he stopped by my turnstile and waited for me to finish my conversation with my coworker.

"Thanks again," he said.

"You should thank me publicly tonight at your concert," I joked.

"Are you coming?"

"I've had my ticket since the first day they went on sale."

I swear I saw him blush. "Well, hopefully, I'll see you later…" He paused to read my nametag. "…Miss Crystal." He pulled a piece of paper from the pocket of his hoodie and handed it to me.

*A V.I.P. pass?* I thought, while accepting the paper that was too flimsy to be anything important. After staring at the receipt that listed his purchases from T.I.S. Bookstore, I looked blankly at him.

"You want me to be your trash girl, too?" I asked.

"What?"

I shook my head and threw the receipt in the can near my foot. "Anything else you need before you go, Your Majesty?" I'd heard he was a little cocky, but if I was expected to perform one more favor, I was going to remind him that I wasn't on the payroll to be his little bitch.

"How are you gonna call me when my number's in the trash?" he asked before licking his lips and walking away.

That was fourteen years ago, and to this day, Dante still denies licking his lips like a lame. I tell him he ought to try licking 'em nowadays so I can feel what I felt that day. Realistically, though, the newness of love or lust can't be reenacted or rekindled. It can only be remembered.

Dana's elbow dug into the side of my arm as the girl Dante was serenading planted a kiss on his forehead. She still doesn't understand how I deal with that type of activity. I don't understand either, but as one of the other industry wives told me, it's not to be understood. It's just the way it is. We can either get mad about a chick who fantasizes about having him as her man or smile because we are living out her fantasy.

I can use the line "I know who he's coming home to", but that doesn't mean he's being faithful before he comes home. If our marriage had a theme song, it'd be a cross between MoKenStef's "He's Mine" and Monica's "Sideline Ho". Unlike the songs, though, he keeps his little floozies in check. I told him that he doesn't have to fess up to his extramarital activities, but it'll be on if I see some shit in the tabloids, hear it amongst his band members, or smell it when he comes home. Yes, I said smell it. According to our agreement, he shouldn't even be close enough to *it* to pick up its scent.

While we dated in college, he was very upfront with me. He wanted me to be his girl, but he warned me of his groupies, saying they were a part of the after-party experience just like bottle-popping and dancing. In other words, in his mind, his flings with them didn't count as cheating. I rolled with that for a while, because when it came down to it, I was damn near running a mini soup kitchen during the times I needed to get one off, and I had a list of customers who wanted to feast on a little Cream of Crystal. If men can say "sucking ain't fucking", then women can surely say "eating ain't cheating". I barely saw him anyway because he was living in L.A. and constantly doing promotional shows all over the country. With both of us having needs, we fulfilled them until we could be together again.

Once we became an official couple, we modified our agreement. His after-party experience could no longer involve penetration. Something had to be mine. Something had to be sacred. And I chose Junior, the nickname I had given his eight-incher.

"You don't have a thing to prove," I told him. "If you can't say no to those thirsty hoes, you let 'em drink and that's where it ends. Be about self." He knew exactly what I meant.

Sounds stupid, right? Sure, it was a tough pill to swallow, but when I started going on tour with him and meeting the wives of the other singers, they gave me the water to help get it down. Farah gave me the clearest perspective. In a nutshell, she said a man is only going to say no so many times to half-naked or completely naked girls who meet him at his hotel. Some hoes, like puppies, wait anxiously for their chance to do a trick so they can get a treat. Others, like vultures, are bold enough to attack until they get what they want—a celebrity name to add to their list. Whatever the approach, they usually attain their goal.

"Don't take it personal unless he gets personal," Farah advised. "The problems arise when those tramps feel like they're significant."

Before we tied the knot, Dante and I sat down again for some real talk. I told him I'm no one's fool. Even though his intentions may not be to cheat, shit happens, and I wanted him to be clear on what type of shit was permitted and what wasn't. I laid out the rules under a "deal or no deal" contract. No kissing.

No holding. No real conversation. No number exchanging. No sexing. No repeats. When getting head, he is to wear a condom. No one gets all of him except me. He pleases no one but me.

Of course, he said he was done with that stuff—that he would only be hooking his boys up with a little trim from then on. I can't say if he has or hasn't, but I *can* say I'm smart enough to know better. He's smart enough not to track his dirt through our house, though, and if I don't see it, it isn't happening.

One may ask how a college-educated woman can involve herself in such a situation. Quite frankly, millions of other college-educated women who are married to average, everyday men are in the same predicament. They just choose to turn a blind eye to their man's actions—their damn near poor-ass man's actions. Let me clarify. I'm not even close to being a gold digger. But if I'm going to spend some nights alone while my man is out doing whatever, you better believe I'll be doing so from the comfort of my eight-bedroom mansion, while watching *Cheaters* on the flat-screen TV and soaking in my Jacuzzi tub.

"You have to be one of the strongest women I know," Dana said as the song ended and the girl exited the stage. "The way she looked at him…"

"They all look, sweetie. That's all they can do. It's like shopping at Saks with an EBT card. What the hell you gon' get?"

"You and your analogies," Milky said, smiling and shaking her head.

Once the show was over, me and the girls hit the club to attend my baby's after-party. Dana was killing 'em in her dress, looking like neither a mother nor a teacher. Ironically, she ran into a guy she went to high school with who was fine as early morning snow, could dance his ass off, and spent almost the entire night dancing with her. While Milky and I lounged in V.I.P., she stayed downstairs with him until almost closing time.

Around three a.m., my stomach started feeling queasy, so I made my way over to Dante.

"I'm about to go back to the hotel, baby. What you wanna do?" I said in his ear, while caressing his neck on the opposite side.

"I got you, baby," he replied before giving me a kiss goodbye. He knew then he only had about an hour and a half window to make it to the room and get some before I passed out.

I gathered the girls and we headed to the valet station.

"You look like you're gonna throw up," Milky said as we waited near the curb.

"I feel like it, too." I looked at Dana, who was fiddling with her phone. "What you doin' over there? Texting Mr. High School?"

"Girl, please. Not at all."

I twisted my lips in disbelief.

"I don't even have his number," she added.

"You're on punishment. How you gon' wear the fuck-'em-girl dress and not do your thing?"

"Probably because she's wearing that ring," Milky said, pointing to Dana's left finger.

"Right!" Dana agreed. "I did exactly what I wanted to do. I had a ball celebrating my renewed sexiness. You know I wasn't trying to walk away with anybody tonight. I wanted to forget about Ric being an inconsiderate idiot, not forget that he's my husband."

All I could do was shrug as the valet parked the car in front of us. "Let's roll, ladies."

When we got back to the room, I flipped the light switch, and Dana instantly gasped.

"Flowers!" Dana's high came down just as quickly as it went up. She walked past the table where they set and plopped onto the bed. "I know they aren't for me. Ric and I were dating the last time I got flowers."

"Shut up, fool," I said with a chuckle. "Bet Mr. High School would give you flowers."

She threw one of her heels in my direction. I dodged it and pulled the card from the plastic holder to read it. "To Willow...From Vaughn...Just Because."

"Awww!" Dana sang as she lay with the pillow covering her head. "Forget y'all and your cutesy marriages."

Milky admired the flowers as I let Vaughn's words sink in. "Ain't that special. The card should've read, 'Just because I went upside your head again'." I flicked a petal before going into the bathroom. "Please."

I didn't have to pee, but I found it best to retreat to avoid embarrassing my sister any further. Dana is like a sister to us, as well, so she knows the situation. Still,

I like to save my verbal thrashings for when Milky and I are in private.

She didn't think I knew this time. She was flitting around backstage and at the after-party like she was all good, but I saw the hint of bruising just above her cheekbone. I told her the last time it happened that if he even thought about laying his hands on her again in any way other than seductively, I was saying something. She begs me to stay out of it, but I'm not sure how long I can keep my mouth shut.

I exited the bathroom, only to find Dana knocked out and Milky texting on her phone. There was no question of who was on the other end of that chat.

"Alright, I'm gone. I'll see y'all in the morning."

Since she was pissed, Milky didn't acknowledge me, and I didn't make time to call her out. I would have plenty of time to do that the next day. My priority was getting to my room and taking some Pepto Bismol before Dante came back and rocked my body into a seasick frenzy...hopefully.

**want more
PORTIA A. COSBY?**

TOO LITTLE, TOO LATE
LESSON LEARNED: IT IS WHAT IT IS
THE DISGRUNTLED WIVES CLUB
IT'S COMPLICATED

*www.portiaacosby.com*